Bayard Taylor, John Lord

**Two German giants: Frederic the Great and Bismarck**

The founder and the builder of German empire

Bayard Taylor, John Lord

**Two German giants: Frederic the Great and Bismarck**
*The founder and the builder of German empire*

ISBN/EAN: 9783337274788

Printed in Europe, USA, Canada, Australia, Japan

Cover: Foto ©Raphael Reischuk / pixelio.de

More available books at **www.hansebooks.com**

# Two German Giants:

## FREDERIC THE GREAT
## AND BISMARCK.

### THE FOUNDER AND THE BUILDER OF GERMAN EMPIRE.

BY

## JOHN LORD. D.D., LL.D.,

*Author of    Beacon Lights of History," etc.*

TO WHICH ARE ADDED

*A CHARACTER SKETCH OF BISMARCK BY BAYARD TAYLOR AND BISMARCK'S GREAT SPEECH ON THE ENLARGE-MENT OF THE GERMAN ARMY IN 1888.*

## With Two Portraits.

NEW YORK :
FORDS, HOWARD, & HULBERT.
1894.

# PUBLISHERS' NOTE.

THE closing of the career of Germany's great Chancellor marks an epoch in European history. The consolidation and extension to imperial proportions of the Prussian Power, founded by the warlike Frederic, has been completed by the colossal hand of Bismarck. It has been a wonderful drama, the life and soul of which are to be found in the personality, the force, genius, and heroism, of the chief actors.

As a modern Plutarch, Dr. John Lord has been enlightening a multitude of readers with spirited biographies of the men and women who stand for great movements in the world's progress; and in the long line of his studies it were difficult to find more striking characters than these two giants, who founded and builded the German Empire. The lecture on Frederic's career (1712–1786) is here followed by the one on Bismarck, whose story, however, is prefaced by the achievements of Stein, Hardenberg, and Scharnhorst, practically filling in the time between the two. If in these lectures history seems to dominate biography, it will be remembered that the men made the history, and it is a

part of their lives. While placing a high estimate on
the immense services of each to the State, Dr. Lord is
open-eyed to the crime of the one and the arrogance of
the other. He is especially amazed that Carlyle, with
all his hatred of shams, should have tried to "cover
up with sophistries" the crimes of Frederic ; and with
incisive pen he impartially notes the foibles and faults
as well as the grand traits of the Iron Chancellor.

By way of completing the conception of Bismarck,
there has been added a character sketch of him, written
by Bayard Taylor, shortly after returning from his post
as United States Minister to Germany. This is valuable for its discriminating analysis of Bismarck, both as
politician and as statesman, while enlivened by personal
reminiscences and anecdotes illustrating the character-
istics of the man.

No discussion of Bismarck's life and policy would be
fair without giving full weight to his convictions concerning the maintenance of the immense military organization that Germany is carrying. In the lecture
on Frederic, Dr. Lord reprobates the ambition of Prussia for military aggrandizement, yet sees a possible
justification of it in providing a barrier against the
barbarous irruption of Russia into Europe; while Bismarck's realization of that and other dangers threatening
Germany—situated in the midst of jealous rivals and
making herself too strong to be successfully attacked—
has compelled the author's qualified approbation. Dr.
Lord makes direct reference, on this point, to the speech
—or rather the familiar and witty talk, for Bismarck's
eloquence was essentially practical and, like his conduct

of life, contemptuous of formality—delivered to the
Reichstag in 1888, while the bill for larger armament
and moneys to support it was under discussion. This
speech has been also added, as essential to a just understanding of Bismarck's policy. It is a résumé of the
relations of Germany to the rest of Europe, unmatched
for graphic condensation,—as Bismarck himself calls
it, "a forty years' tableau."

Frederic and Bismarck, these two rugged chieftains,
the real creators of the German Fatherland, are set
forth in the stirring sentences of Dr. Lord and the
critical narrative of Bayard Taylor in their own peculiar
personalities. And it is believed that, without pretence
of exhaustive, detailed history, this brief book will give
a just and lucid view of the parts they played in war,
diplomacy, and statecraft, which have shaped the life of
Germany and profoundly affected the course of continental Europe for two centuries.

# CONTENTS.

vii

# PORTRAITS.

# FREDERIC THE GREAT.

## THE PRUSSIAN POWER.

FRÉDÉRIC II.

# FREDERIC THE GREAT.

## THE PRUSSIAN POWER.

THE history of Frederic the Great is simply that of a man who committed an outrageous crime, the consequences of which pursued him in the maledictions and hostilities of Europe, and who fought bravely and heroically to rescue himself and country from the ruin which impended over him as a consequence of this crime. His heroism, his fertility of resources, his unflagging energy, and his amazing genius in overcoming difficulties won for him the admiration of that class who idolize strength and success; so that he stands out in history as a struggling gladiator who baffled all his foes, — not a dying gladiator on the arena of a pagan amphitheatre, but more like a Judas Maccabeus, when hunted by the Syrian hosts, rising victorious, and laying the foundation of a powerful monarchy; indeed, his fame spread, irrespective of his cause and character, from one end of Christendom to the other, — not such a fame as endeared Gustavus Adolphus to the heart of

11

nations for heroic efforts to save the Protestant religion, — but such a fame as the successful generals of ancient Rome won by adding territories to a warlike State, regardless of all the principles of right and wrong. Such a career is suggestive of grand moral lessons; and it is to teach these lessons that I describe a character for whom I confess I feel but little sympathy, yet whom I am compelled to respect for his heroic qualities and great abilities.

Frederic of Prussia was born in 1712, and had an unhappy childhood and youth from the caprices of a royal but disagreeable father, best known for his tall regiment of guards; a severe, austere, prejudiced, formal, narrow, and hypochondriacal old Pharisee, whose sole redeeming excellence was an avowed belief in God Almighty and in the orthodox doctrines of the Protestant Church.

In 1740, this rigid, exacting, unsympathetic king died; and his son Frederic, who had been subjected to the severest discipline, restraints, annoyances, and humiliations, ascended the throne, and became the third King of Prussia, at the age of twenty-eight. His kingdom was a small one, being then about one quarter of its present size.

And here we pause for a moment to give a glance at the age in which he lived, — an age of great reactions, when the stirring themes and issues of the seventeenth

century were substituted for mockeries, levities, and
infidelities; when no fierce protests were made except
those of Voltaire against the Jesuits; when an aban-
doned woman ruled France, as the mistress of an
enervated monarch; when Spain and Italy were sunk
in lethargic forgetfulness, Austria was priest-ridden,
and England was governed by a ring of selfish landed
proprietors; when there was no marked enterprise but
the slave-trade; when no department of literature or
science was adorned by original genius; and when
England had no broader statesman than Walpole, no
abler churchman than Warburton, no greater poet than
Pope. There was a general indifference to lofty speculation. A materialistic philosophy was in fashion,—
not openly atheistic, but arrogant and pretentious, whose
only power was in sarcasm and mockery, like the satires
of Lucian, extinguishing faith, godless and yet boastful,
— an Epicureanism such as Socrates attacked and Paul
rebuked. It found its greatest exponent in Voltaire,
the oracle and idol of intellectual Europe. In short,
it was an age when general cynicism and reckless
abandonment to pleasure marked the upper-classes; an
age which produced Chesterfield, as godless a man as
Voltaire himself.

In this period of religious infidelity, moral torpor,
fashionable mediocrity, unthinking pleasure-seeking,
and royal orgies; when the people were spurned, in-

sulted and burdened, — Frederic ascends an absolute throne. He is a young and fashionable philosopher. He professes to believe in nothing that ages of inquiry and study are supposed to have settled; he even ridicules the religious principles of his father. He ardently adopts everything which claims to be a novelty, but is not learned enough to know that what he supposes to be new has been exploded over and over again. He is liberal and tolerant, but does not see the logical sequence of the very opinions he indorses. He is also what is called an accomplished man, since he can play on an instrument, and amuse a dinner-party by jokes and stories. He builds a magnificent theatre, and collects statues, pictures, snuff-boxes, and old china. He welcomes to his court, not stern thinkers, but sneering and amusing philosophers. He employs in his service both Catholics and Protestants alike, since he holds in contempt the religion of both. He is free from animosities and friendships, and neither punishes those who are his enemies nor rewards those who are his friends. He apes reform, but shackles the press; he appoints able men in his service, but cnly those who will be his unscrupulous tools. He has a fine physique, and therefore is unceasingly active. He flies from one part of his kingdom to another, not to examine morals or education or the state of the people, but to inspect lortresses and to collect camps.

To such a man the development of the resources of his kingdom, the reform of abuses, and educational projects are of secondary importance; he gives his primary attention to raising and equipping armies, having in view the extension of his kingdom by aggressive and unjustifiable wars. He cares little for domestic joys or the society of women, and is incapable of sincere friendship. He has no true admiration for intellectual excellence, although he patronizes literary lions. He is incapable of any sacrifice except for his troops, who worship him, since their interests are identical with his own. In the camp or in the field he spends his time, amusing himself occasionally with the society of philosophers as cynical as himself. He has dreams and visions of military glory, which to him is the highest and greatest on this earth, Charles XII. being his model of a hero.

With such views he enters upon a memorable career. His first important public act as king is the seizure of part of the territory of the Bishop of Liège, which he claims as belonging to Prussia. The old bishop is indignant and amazed, but is obliged to submit to a robbery which disgusts Christendom, but is not of sufficient consequence to set it in a blaze.

The next thing he does, of historical importance, is to seize Silesia, a province which belongs to Austria, and contains about twenty thousand square miles, — a fertile and beautiful province, nearly as large as his own kingdom; it is the highest table-land of Germany, girt around with mountains, hard to attack and easy to defend. So rapid and secret are his movements, that this unsuspecting and undefended country is overrun by his veteran soldiers as easily as Louis XIV. overran Flanders and Holland, and with no better excuse than the French king had. This outrage was an open insult to Europe, as well as a great wrong to Maria Theresa, — supposed by him to be a feeble woman who could not resent the injury. But in this woman he found the great enemy of his life, — a lioness deprived of her whelps, whose wailing was so piteous and so savage that she aroused Europe from lethargy, and made coalitions which shook it to its centre. At first she simply rallied her own troops, and fought single-handed to recover her lost and most valued province. But Frederic, with marvellous celerity and ability, got possession of the Silesian fortresses; the bloody battle of Mollwitz (1741) secured his prey, and he returned in triumph to his capital, to abide the issue of events.

It is not easy to determine whether this atrocious crime, which astonished Europe, was the result of his early passion for military glory, or the inauguration of a policy of aggression and aggrandizement. But it was the signal of an explosion of European politics which ended in one of the most bloody wars of modern times. "It was," says Carlyle, "the little stone broken loose from the mountain, hitting others, big and little, which again hit others with their leaping and rolling, till the whole mountain-side was in motion under law of gravity."

Maria Theresa appeals to her Hungarian nobles, with her infant in her arms, at a diet of the nation, and sends her envoys to every friendly court. She offers her unscrupulous enemy the Duchy of Limberg and two hundred thousand pounds to relinquish his grasp on Silesia. It is like the offer of Darius to Alexander, and is spurned by the Prussian robber. It is not Limberg he wants, nor money, but Silesia, which he resolves to keep because he wants it, and at any hazard, even were he to jeopardize his own hereditary dominions. The peace of Breslau gives him a temporary leisure, and he takes the waters of Aachen, and discusses philosophy. He is uneasy, but jubilant, for he has nearly doubled the territory and population of Prussia. His subjects proclaim him a hero, with immense pæans. Doubtless, too, he now desires peace, — just as Louis XIV. did after he had conquered Holland, and as Napoleon did when he had seated his brothers on the old thrones of Europe.

But there can be no lasting peace after such outrageous wickedness. The angered kings and princes of Europe are to become the instruments of eternal

justice. They listen to the eloquent cries of the
Austrian Empress, and prepare for war, to punish the
audacious robber who disturbs the peace of the world
and insults all other nationalities. But they are not
yet ready for effective war; the storm does not at
once break out.

The Austrians however will not wait, and the second
S:        .var ensues, in which Saxony joins Austria.
Again is Frederic successful, over the combined forces
of these two powers, and he retains his stolen province.
He is now regarded as a world-hero, for he has fought
bravely against vastly superior forces, and is received
in Berlin with unbounded enthusiasm. He renews his
studies in philosophy, courts literary celebrities, re-
organizes his army, and collects forces for a renewed
encounter, which he foresees.

He has ten years of repose and preparation, during
which he is lauded and flattered, yet retaining sim-
plicity of habits, sleeping but five hours a day, finding
time for state dinners, flute-playing, and operas, of all
which he is fond; for he was doubtless a man of cul-
ture, social, well read if not profound, witty, inquiring,
and without any striking defects save tyranny, ambition, parsimony, dissimulation, and lying.

It was during those ten years of rest and military
preparation that Voltaire made his memorable visit —
his third and last — to Pottsdam and Berlin, thirty-two

months of alternate triumph and humiliation. No literary man ever had so successful and brilliant a career as this fortunate and lauded Frenchman,— the oracle of all salons, the arbiter of literary fashions, a dictator in the realm of letters, with amazing fecundity of genius directed into all fields of labor; poet, historian, dramatist, and philosopher; writing books enough to load a cart, and all of them admired and extolled, all of them scattered over Europe, read by all nations; a marvellous worker, of unbounded wit and unexampled popularity, whose greatest literary merit was in the transcendent excellence of his style, for which chiefly he is immortal; a great artist, rather than an original and profound genius whose ideas form the basis of civilizations. The King of Prussia formed an ardent friendship for this king of letters, based on admiration rather than respect; invited him to his court, extolled and honored him, and lavished on him all that he could bestow, outside of political distinction. But no worldly friendship could stand such a test as both were subjected to, since they at last comprehended each other's character and designs. Voltaire perceived the tyranny, the ambition, the heartlessness, the egotism, and the exactions of his royal patron, and despised him while he flattered him; and Frederic on his part saw the hollowness, the meanness, the suspicion, the irritability, the pride, the insincerity, the tricks, the ingratitude, the baseness, the lies of his distinguished guest, — and their friendship ended in utter vanity. What friendship can last without mutual respect? The friendship of Frederic and Voltaire was hopelessly broken, in spite of the remembrance of mutual admiration and happy hours. It was patched up and mended like a broken vase, but it could not be restored. How sad, how mournful, how humiliating is a broken friendship or an alienated love! It is the falling away of the foundations of the soul, the disappearance forever of what is most to be prized on earth, — its celestial certitudes. A beloved friend may die, but we are consoled in view of the fact that the friendship may be continued in heaven: the friend is not lost to us. But when a friendship or a love is broken, there is no continuance of it through eternity. It is the gloomiest thing to think of in this whole world.

But Frederic was too busy and pre-occupied a man to mourn long for a departed joy. He was absorbed in preparations for war. The sword of Damocles was suspended over his head, and he knew it better than any other man in Europe; he knew it from his spies and emissaries. Though he had enjoyed ten years' peace, he knew that peace was only a truce; that the nations were arming in behalf of the injured empress; that so great a crime as the seizure of Silesia must be visited with a penalty; that there was no escape for him except in a tremendous life-and-death struggle, which was to be the trial of his life; that defeat was more than probable, since the forces in preparation against him were overwhelming. The curses of the civilized world still pursued him, and in his retreat at Sans Souci he had no rest; and hence he became irritable and suspicious. The clouds of the political atmosphere were filled with thunderbolts, ready to fall upon him and crush him at any moment; indeed, nothing could arrest the long-gathering storm.

It broke out with unprecedented fury in the spring of 1756. Austria, Russia, Sweden, Saxony, and France were combined to ruin him, — the most powerful coalition of the European powers seen since the Thirty Years' War. His only ally was England, — an ally not so much to succor him as to humble France, and hence her aid was timid and incompetent.

Thus began the famous Seven Years' War, during which France lost her colonial possessions, and was signally humiliated at home, — a war which developed the genius of the elder Pitt, and placed England in the proud position of mistress of the ocean; a war marked by the largest array of forces which Europe had seen since the times of Charles V., in which six hundred thousand men were marshalled under different leaders and nations, to crush a man who had insulted Europe and defied the law of nations and the laws of God. The coalition represented one hundred millions of people with inexhaustible resources.

Now, it was the memorable resistance of Frederic II. to this vast array of forces, and his successful retention of the province he had seized, which gave him his chief claim as a hero; and it was his patience, his fortitude, his energy, his fertility of resources, and the enthusiasm with which he inspired his troops even after the most discouraging and demoralizing defeats, that won for him that universal admiration as a man which he lived to secure in spite of all his defects and crimes.  We admire the resources and dexterity of an outlawed bandit, but we should remember he is a bandit still; and we confound all the laws which hold society together, when we cover up the iniquity of a great crime by the successes which have apparently baffled justice. Frederic II., by stealing Silesia, and thus provoking a great war of untold and indescribable miseries, is entitled to anything but admiration, whatever may have been his military genius; and I am amazed that so great a man as Carlyle, with all his hatred of shams, and his clear perceptions of justice and truth, should have whitewashed such a robber.  I cannot conceive how the severest critic of the age should have spent the best years of his life in apologies for so bad a man, if his own philosophy had not become radically unsound, based on the abominable doctrine that the end justifies the means, and that an outward success is the test of right. Far different was Carlyle's treatment of Cromwell. Frederic had no such cause as Cromwell; it was simply his own or his country's aggrandizement by any means, or by any sword he could lay hold of. The chief merit of Carlyle's history is his impartiality and accuracy in describing the details of the contest: the cause of the contest he does not sufficiently reprobate; and all his sympathies seem to be with the unscrupulous robber who fights heroically, rather than with indignant Europe outraged by his crimes. But we cannot separate crime from its consequences; and all the reverses, the sorrows, the perils, the hardships, the humiliations, the immense losses, the dreadful calamities through which Prussia had to pass, which wrung even the heart of Frederic with anguish, were only a merited retribution. The Seven Years' War was a king-hunt, in which all the forces of the surrounding monarchies gathered around the doomed man, making his circle smaller and smaller, and which would certainly have ended in his utter ruin, had he not been rescued by events as unexpected as they were unparalleled. Had some great and powerful foe been converted suddenly into a friend at a critical moment, Napoleon, another unscrupulous robber, might not have been defeated at Waterloo, or died on a rock in the ocean. But Providence, it would seem, who rules the fate of war, had some inscrutable reason for the rescue of Prussia under Frederic, and the humiliation of France under Napoleon.

The brunt of the war fell of course upon Austria, so that, as the two nations were equally German, it had many of the melancholy aspects of a civil war. But Austria was Catholic and Prussia was Protestant; and had Austria succeeded, Germany possibly to-day would have been united under an irresistible Catholic imperialism, and there would have been no German empire whose capital is Berlin. The Austrians, in this contest, fought bravely and ably, under Prince Carl and Marshal Daun, who were no mean competitors with the King of Prussia for military laurels. But the Austrians fought on the offensive, and the Prussians on the defensive. The former were obliged to manœuvre on the circumference, the latter in the centre of the circle. The Austrians, in order to recover Silesia, were compelled to cross high mountains whose passes were guarded by Prussian soldiers. The war began in offensive operations, and ended in defensive.

The most terrible enemy that Frederic had, next to Austria, was Russia, ruled then by Elizabeth, who had the deepest sympathy with Maria Theresa; but when she died, affairs took a new turn. Frederic was then on the very verge of ruin, — was, as they say, about to be "bagged," — when the new Emperor of Russia conceived a great personal admiration for his genius and heroism; the Russian enmity was converted to friendship, and the Czar became an ally instead of a foe.

The aid which the Saxons gave to Maria Theresa availed but little. The population, chiefly and traditionally Protestant, probably sympathized with Prussia more than with Austria, although the King himself was Catholic,—that inglorious monarch who resembled in his gallantries Louis XV., and in his dilettante tastes Leo X. He is chiefly known for the number of his concubines and his Dresden gallery of pictures.

The aid which the French gave was really imposing, so far as numbers make efficient armies. But the French were not the warlike people in the reign of Louis XV. that they were under Henry IV., or Napoleon Bonaparte. They fought, without the stimulus of national enthusiasm, without a cause, as part of a great machine. They never have been successful in war without the inspiration of a beloved cause. This war had no especial attraction or motive for them. What was it to Frenchmen, so absorbed with themselves, whether a Hohenzollern or a Hapsburg reigned in Germany? Hence, the great armies which the government of France sent to the aid of Maria Theresa were without spirit, and were not even marshalled by able generals. In fact, the French seemed more intent on crippling England than in crushing Frederic. The war had immense complications. Though France and England were drawn into it, yet both France and England fought more against each other than for the parties who had summoned them to their rescue.

England was Frederic's ally, but her aid was not great directly. She did not furnish him with many troops; she sent subsidies instead, which enabled him to continue the contest. But these were not as great as he expected, or had reason to expect. With all the money he received from Walpole or Pitt he was reduced to the most desperate straits.

One thing was remarkable in that long war of seven years, which strained every nerve and taxed every energy of Prussia: it was carried on by Frederic in hard cash. He did not run in debt; he always had enough on hand in coin to pay for all expenses. But then his subjects were most severely taxed, and the soldiers were poorly paid. If the same economy he used in that war of seven years had been exercised by our Government in its late war, we should not have had any national debt at all at the close of the war, although we probably should have suspended specie payments.

It would not be easy or interesting to attempt to compress the details of a long war of seven years in a single lecture. The records of war have great uniformity, — devastation, taxes, suffering, loss of life and

of property (except by the speculators and government
agents), the flight of literature, general demoralization,
the lowering of the tone of moral feeling, the ascendency of unscrupulous men, the exaltation of military
talents, general grief at the loss of friends, fiendish
exultation over victories alternated with depressing
despondency in view of defeats, the impoverishment
of a nation on the whole, and the sickening conviction,
which fastens on the mind after the first excitement
is over, of a great waste of life and property for which
there is no return, and which sometimes a whole generation cannot restore. Nothing is so dearly purchased
as the laurels of the battle-field; nothing is so great
a delusion and folly as military glory to the eye of a
Christian or philosopher. It is purchased by the tears
and blood of millions, and is rebuked by all that is
grand in human progress. Only degraded and demoralized peoples can ever rejoice in war; and when it is
not undertaken for a great necessity, it fills the world
with bitter imprecations. It is cruel and hard and
unjust in its nature, and utterly antagonistic to civilization. Its greater evils are indeed overruled; Satan
is ever rebuked and baffled by a benevolent Providence. But war is always a curse and a calamity in its
immediate results, — and in its ultimate results also,
unless waged in defence of some immortal cause.

It must be confessed, war is terribly exciting. The

eyes of the civilized world were concentrated on Frederic II. during this memorable period; and most people
anticipated his overthrow.   They read everywhere of his
marchings and counter-marchings,. his sieges and battles, his hair-breadth escapes, and his renewed exertions,
from the occupation of Saxony to the battle of Torgau.
In this war he was sometimes beaten, as at Kolin; but
he gained three memorable victories, — one over the
French, at Rossbach; the second, over the Austrians,
at Luthen; and the third, over the Russians, at Zorn-
dorf, the most bloody of all his battles.   And he gained
these victories by outflanking, his attack being the form
of a wedge, — learned by the example of Epaminondas,
— a device which led to new tactics, and proclaimed
Frederic a master of the art of war.   But in these
battles he simply showed himself to be a great general.
It was not until his reverses came that he showed
himself a great man, or earned the sympathy which
Europe felt for a humiliated monarch, putting forth
herculean energies to save his crown and kingdom.
His easy and great victories in the first year of the war
simply saved him from annihilation; they were not
great enough to secure peace.   Although thus far he
was a conqueror, he had no peace, no rest, and but
little hope.   His enemies were so numerous and powerful that they could send large reinforcements: he could
draw but few.   In time it was apparent that he would

be destroyed, whatever his skill and bravery. Had not
the Empress Elizabeth died, he would have been conquered and prostrated. After his defeat at Hochkirch,
he was obliged to dispute his ground inch by inch,
compelled to hide his grief from his soldiers, financially
straitened and utterly forlorn; but for a timely subsidy
from England he would have been desperate. The fatal
battle of Kunnersdorf, in his fourth campaign, when
he lost twenty thousand men, almost drove him to despair; and evil fortune continued to pursue him in his
fifth campaign, in which he lost some of his strongest
fortresses, and Silesia was opened to his enemies. At
one time he had only six days' provisions: the world
marvelled how he held out. Then England deserted
him. He made incredible exertions to avert his doom:
everlasting marches, incessant perils; no comforts or
luxuries as a king, only sorrows, privations, sufferings;
enduring more labors than his soldiers; with restless
anxieties and blasted hopes. In his despair and humiliation it is said he recognized God Almighty. In
his chastisements and misfortunes, — apparently on the
very brink of destruction, and with the piercing cries
of misery which reached his ears from every corner of
his dominions, — he must, at least, have recognized a
Retribution. Still his indomitable will remained. His
pride and his self-reliance never deserted him; he would
have died rather than have yielded up Silesia until

wrested from him.   At last the battle of Torgau, fought
in the night, and the death of the Empress of Russia,
removed the overhanging clouds, and he was enabled
to contend with Austria unassisted by France and Russia.   But if Maria Theresa could not recover Silesia,
aided by the great monarchies of Europe, what could
she do without their aid ?   So peace came at last, when
all parties were wearied and exhausted ; and Frederic
retained his stolen province at the sacrifice of one hundred and eighty thousand men, and the decline of one
tenth of the whole population of his kingdom and its
complete impoverishment, from which it did not recover for nearly one hundred years.   Prussia, though a
powerful military state, became and remained one of
the poorest countries of Europe ; and I can remember
when it was rare to see there, except in the houses of
the rich, either a silver fork or a silver spoon ; to say
nothing of the cheap and frugal fare of the great mass
of the people, and their comfortless kind of life, with
hardly any physical luxuries except tobacco and beer.
It is surprising how, in a poor country, Frederic could
have sustained such an exhaustive war without in-
curring a national debt.   Perhaps it was not as easy
in those times for kings and states to run into debt
as it is now.   One of the great refinements of advancing civilization is that we are permitted to bequeath .
our burdens to future generations.   Time only will

show whether this is the wisest course. It is certainly
not a wise thing for individuals to do. He who enters
on the possession of a heavily mortgaged estate is an
embarrassed, perhaps impoverished, man. Frederic, at
least, did not leave debts for posterity to pay; he
preferred to pay as he went along, whatever were
the difficulties.

The real gainer by the war, if gainer there was, was
England, since she was enabled to establish a maritime
supremacy, and develop her manufacturing and mer-
cantile resources, — much needed in her future struggles
to resist Napoleon. She also gained colonial possessions, a foothold in India, and the possession of Canada.
This war entangled Europe, and led to great battles,
not in Germany merely, but around the world. It was
during this war, when France and England were antagonistic forces, that the military genius of Washington
was first developed in America. The victories of Clive
and Hastings soon after followed in India.

The greatest loser in this war was France: she lost
provinces and military prestige. The war brought to
light the decrepitude of the Bourbon rule. The marshals of France, with superior forces, were disgracefully
defeated. The war plunged France in debt, only to be
paid by a " roaring conflagration of anarchies." The
logical sequence of the war was in those discontents
and taxes which prepared the way for the French

Revolution, — a catastrophe or a new birth, as men differently view it.

The effect of the war on Austria was a loss of prestige, the beginning of the dismemberment of the empire, and the revelation of internal weakness. Though Maria Theresa gained general sympathy, and won great glory by her vigorous government and the heroism of her troops, she was a great loser. Besides the loss of men and money, Austria ceased to be the great threatening power of Europe. From this war England, until the close of the career of Napoleon, was really the most powerful state in Europe, and became the proudest.

As for Prussia, — the principal transgressor and actor, — it is more difficult to see the actual results. The immediate effects of the war were national impoverishment, an immense loss of life, and a fearful demoralization. The limits of the kingdom were enlarged, and its military and political power was established. It became one of the leading states of Continental Europe, surpassed only by Austria, Russia, and France. It led to great standing armies and a desire of aggrandizement. It made the army the centre of all power and the basis of social prestige. It made Frederic II. the great military hero of that age, and perpetuated his policy in Prussia. Bismarck is the sequel and sequence of Frederic. It was by aggressive and unscrupulous wars that the Romans were aggrandized, and it was also by the habits and tastes which successful war created that Rome was ultimately undermined. The Roman empire did not last like the Chinese empire, although at one period it had more glory and prestige. So war both strengthens and impoverishes nations. But I believe that the violation of eternal principles of right ultimately brings a fearful penalty. It may be long delayed, but it will finally come, as in the sequel of the wicked wars of Louis XIV. and Napoleon Bonaparte. Victor Hugo, in his " History of a Great Crime," on the principle of everlasting justice, forewarned "Napoleon the Little" of his future reverses, while nations and kingdoms, in view of his marvellous successes, hailed him as a friend of civilization; and Hugo lived to see the fulfilment of his prophecy. Moreover, it may be urged that the Prussian people, — ground down by an absolute military despotism, the mere tools of an ambitious king, — were not responsible for the atrocious conquests of Frederic II. The misrule of monarchs does not bring permanent degradation on a nation, unless it shares the crimes of its monarch, — as in the case of the Romans, when the leading idea of the people was military conquest, from the very commencement of their state. The Prussians in the time of Frederic were a sincere, patriotic, and religious people. They were simply enslaved, and suffered the poverty and misery which were entailed by war.

After Frederic had escaped the perils of the Seven Years' War, it is surprising he should so soon have become a party to another atrocious crime, — the division and dismemberment of Poland. But here both Russia and Austria were also participants.

"Sarmatia fell, unwept, without a crime."

And I am still more amazed that Carlyle should cover up this crime with his sophistries. No man in ordinary life would be justified in seizing his neighbor's property because he was weak and his property was mismanaged. We might as well justify Russia in attempting to seize Turkey, although such a crime may be overruled in the future good of Europe. But Carlyle is an Englishman; and the English seized and conquered India because they wanted it, not because they had a right to it. The same laws which bind individuals also binds kings and nations. Free nations from the obligations which bind individuals, and the world would be an anarchy. Grant that Poland was not fit for self-government, this does not justify its political annihilation. The heart of the world exclaimed against that crime at the time, and the injuries of that unfortunate state are not yet forgotten. Carlyle says the "partition of Poland was an operation of Almighty Providence and the eternal laws of Nature," — a key to his whole philosophy, which means,

if it means anything, that as great fishes swallow up
the small ones, and wild beasts prey upon each other,
and eagles and vultures devour other birds, it is all
right for powerful nations to absorb the weak ones,
as the Romans did. Might does not make right by
the eternal decrees of God Almighty, written in the
Bible and on the consciences of mankind. Politicians,
whose primal law is expediency, may justify such acts
as public robbery, for they are political Jesuits, — always were, always will be; and even calm statesmen,
looking on the overruling of events, may palliate; but
to enlightened Christians there is only one law, "Do
unto others as ye would that they should do unto you."
Nor can Christian civilization reach an exalted plane
until it is in harmony with the eternal laws of God.
Mr. Carlyle glibly speaks of Almighty Providence
favoring robbery; here he utters a falsehood, and I
do not hesitate to say it, great as is his authority.
God says, "Thou shalt not steal; Thou shalt not
covet anything which is thy neighbor's, . . . for he is
a jealous God, visiting the sins of the fathers upon
the children, to the third and fourth generation."
We must set aside the whole authority of divine
revelation, to justify any crime openly or secretly committed. The prosperity of nations, in the long run, is
based on righteousness; not on injustice, cruelty, and
selfishness.

It cannot be denied that Frederic well managed his stolen property. He was a man of ability, of enlightened views, of indefatigable industry, and of an iron will. I would as soon deny that Cromwell did not well govern the kingdom which he had seized, on the plea of revolutionary necessity and the welfare of England, for he also was able and wise. But what was the fruit of Cromwell's well-intended usurpation? — a hideous reaction, the return of the Stuarts, the dissipation of his visionary dreams. And if the states which Frederic seized, and the empire he had founded in blood and carnage had been as well prepared for liberty as England was, the consequences of his ambition might have been far different.

But Frederic did not so much aim at the development of national resources, — the aim of all immortal statesmen, — as at the growth and establishment of a military power. He filled his kingdom and provinces with fortresses and camps and standing armies. He cemented a military monarchy. As a wise executive ruler, the King of Prussia enforced law and order, was economical in his expenditures, and kept up a rigid discipline; even rewarded merit, and was friendly to learning. And he showed many interesting personal qualities, — for I do not wish to make him out a monster, only as a great man who did wicked things, and things which even cemented for the time the power of Prussia. He was frugal and unostentatious. Like Charlemagne, he associated with learned men. He loved music and literature; and he showed an amazing fortitude and patience in adversity, which called out universal admiration. He had a great insight into shams, was rarely imposed upon, and was scrupulous and honest in his dealings as an individual. He was also a fascinating man when he unbent; was affable, intelligent, accessible, and unstilted. He was an admirable talker, and a tolerable author. He always sympathized with intellectual excellence. He surrounded himself with great men in all departments. He had good taste and a severe dignity, and despised vulgar people; had no craving for fast horses, and held no intercourse with hostlers and gamblers, even if these gamblers had the respectable name of brokers. He punished all public thieves; so that his administration at least was dignified and respectable, and secured the respect of Europe and the admiration of men of ability. The great warrior was also a great statesman, and never made himself ridiculous, never degraded his position and powers, and could admire and detect a man of genius, even when hidden from the world. He was a Tiberius, but not a Nero fiddling over national calamities, and surrounding himself with stage-players, buffoons, and idiots.

But here his virtues ended. He was cold, selfish,

dissembling, hard-hearted, ungrateful, ambitious, unscrupulous, without faith in either God or man; so
sceptical in religion that he was almost an atheist.
He was a disobedient son, a heartless husband, a capricious friend, and a selfish self-idolater.  While he was
the friend of literary men, he patronized those who
were infidel in their creed.  He was not a religious
persecutor, because he regarded all religions as equally
false and equally useful.  He was social among convivial and learned friends, but cared little for women
or female society.  His latter years, though dignified
and quiet, an idol in all military circles, with an immense fame, and surrounded with every pleasure and
luxury at Sans-Souci, were still sad and gloomy, like
those of most great men whose leading principle of
life was vanity and egotism, — like those of Solomon,
Charles V., and Louis XIV.  He heard the distant
rumblings, if he did not live to see the lurid fires, of
the French Revolution.  He had been deceived in
Voltaire, but he could not mistake the logical sequence
of the ideas of Rousseau, — those blasting ideas which
would sweep away all feudal institutions and all irre-
sponsible tyrannies.  When Mirabeau visited him he
was a quaking, suspicious, irritable, capricious, unhappy
old man, though adored by his soldiers to the last, —
for those were the only people he ever loved, those
who were willing to die for him, those who built up

his throne : and when he died, I suppose he was sincerely lamented by his army and his generals and his nobility, for with him began the greatness of Prussia as a military power. So far as a life devoted to the military and political aggrandizement of a country makes a man a patriot, Frederic the Great will receive the plaudits of those men who worship success, and who forget the enormity of unscrupulous crimes in the outward glory which immediately resulted, — yea, possibly of contemplative statesmen who see in the rise of a new power an instrument of the Almighty for some inscrutable end. To me his character and deeds have no fascination, any more than the fortunate career of some one of our modern millionnaires would have to one who took no interest in finance. It was doubtless grateful to the dying King of Prussia to hear the plaudits of his idolaters, as he stood on the hither shores of eternity; but his view of the spectators as they lined those shores must have been soon lost sight of, and their cheering and triumphant voices unheard and disregarded, as the bark, in which he sailed alone, put forth on the unknown ocean, to meet the Eternal Judge of the living and the dead.

We leave now the man who won so great a fame, to consider briefly his influence. In two respects, it seems to me, it has been decided and impressive.

In the first place, he gave an impulse to rationalistic inquiries in Germany; and many there are who think this was a good thing. He made it fashionable to be cynical and doubtful. Being ashamed of his own language, and preferring the French, he encouraged the current and popular French literature, which in his day, under the guidance of Voltaire, was materialistic and deistical. He embraced a philosophy which looked to secondary rather than primal causes, which scouted any revelations that could not be explained by reason, or reconciled with scientific theories, — that false philosophy which intoxicated Franklin and Jefferson as well as Hume and Gibbon, and which finally culminated in Diderot and D'Alembert; the philosophy which became fashionable in German universities, and whose nearest approach was that of the exploded Epicureanism of the Ancients. Under the patronage of the infidel court, the universities of Germany became filled with rationalistic professors, and the pulpits with dead and formal divines; so that the glorious old Lutheranism of Prussia became the coldest and most lifeless of all the forms which Protestantism ever assumed. Doubtless, great critics and scholars arose under the stimulus of that unbounded religious speculation which the King encouraged; but they employed their learning in pulling down rather than supporting the pillars of the ancient orthodoxy. And so rapidly did rationalism spread in Northern Germany, that it changed its great lights into *illuminati,* who spurned what was revealed unless it was in accordance with their speculations and sweeping criticism. I need not dwell on this undisguised and blazing fact, on the rationalism which became the fashion in Germany, and which spread so disastrously over other countries, penetrating even into the inmost sanctuaries of theological instruction. All this may be progress; but to my mind it tended to extinguish the light of faith, and fill the seats of learning with cynics and unbelieving critics. It was bad enough to destroy the bodies of men in a heartless war; it was worse to nourish those principles which poisoned the soul, and spread doubt and disguised infidelities among the learned classes.

But the influence of Frederic was seen in a more marked manner in the inauguration of a national policy directed chiefly to military aggrandizement. If there ever was a purely military monarchy, it is Prussia; and this kingdom has been to Europe what Sparta was to Greece. All the successors of Frederic have followed out his policy with singular tenacity. All their habits and associations have been military. The army has been the centre of their pride, ambition, and hope. They have made their country one vast military camp. They have exempted no classes from military services; they have honored and exalted the army more than

any other interest. The principal people of the land
are generals. The resources of the kingdom are ex-
pended in standing armies; and these are a perpetual
menace. A network of military machinery controls
all other pursuits and interests. The peasant is a
military slave. The student of the university can be
summoned to a military camp. Precedence in rank
is given to military men over merchant princes, over
learned professors, over distinguished jurists. The genius of the nation has been directed to the perfection
of military discipline and military weapons. The government is always prepared for war, and has been
rarely averse to it. It has ever been ready to seize a
province or pick a quarrel. The late war with France
was as much the fault of Prussia as of the government
of Napoleon. The great idea of Prussia is military
aggrandizement; it is no longer a small kingdom, but
a great empire, more powerful than either Austria or
France. It believes in new annexations, until all Germany shall be united under a Prussian Kaiser. What
Rome became, Prussia aspires to be. The spirit, the
animus, of Prussia is military power. Travel in that
kingdom, — everywhere are soldiers, military schools,
camps, arsenals, fortresses, reviews. And this military
spirit, evident during the last hundred years, has made
the military classes arrogant, austere, mechanical, contemptuous. This spirit pervades the nation. It despises

other nations as much as France did in the last century, or England after the wars of Napoleon.

But the great peculiarity of this military spirit is
seen in the large standing armies, which dry up the
resources of the nation and make war a perpetual
necessity, at least a perpetual fear. It may be urged
that these armies are necessary to the protection of the
state, — that if they were disbanded, then France, or
some other power, would arise and avenge their injuries, and cripple a state so potent to do evil. It
may be so; but still the evils generated by these
armies must be fatal to liberty, and antagonistic to
those peaceful energies which produce the highest
civilization. They are fatal to the peaceful virtues.
The great Schiller has said : —

> " There exists
> An higher than the warrior's excellence.
> Great deeds of violence, adventures wild,
> And wonders of the moment, — these are not they
> Which generate the high, the blissful,
> And the enduring majesty.

I do not disdain the virtues which are developed by
war; but great virtues are seldom developed by war,
unless the war is stimulated by love of liberty or the
conservation of immortal privileges worth more than
the fortunes or the lives of men. A nation incapable
of being roused in great necessities soon becomes in-

significant and degenerate, like Greece when it was incorporated with the Roman empire; but I have no admiration of a nation perpetually arming and perpetually seeking political aggrandizement, when the great ends of civilization are lost sight of. And this is what Frederic sought, and his successors who cherished his ideas. The legacy he bequeathed to the world was not emancipating ideas, but the policy of military aggrandizement. And yet, has civilization no higher aim than the imitation of the ancient Romans? Can nations progressively become strong by ignoring the spirit of Christianity? Is a nation only to thrive by adopting the sentiments peculiar to robbers and bandits? I know that Prussia has not neglected education, or science, or industrial energy; but these have been made subservient to military aims. The highest civilization is that which best develops the virtues of the heart and the energies of the mind: on these the strength of man is based. It may be necessary for Prussia, in the complicated relations of governments, and in view of possible dangers, to sustain vast standing armies; but the larger these are, the more do they provoke other nations to do the same, and to eat out the vitals of national wealth. That nation is the greatest which seeks to reduce, rather than augment, forces which prey upon its resources and which are a perpetual menace. And hence the vast standing armies which conquerors seek to maintain are not an aid to civilization, but on the other hand tend to destroy it; unless by civilization and national prosperity are meant an ever-expanding policy of military aggrandizement, by which weaker and unoffending states may be gradually absorbed by irresistible despotism, like that of the Romans, whose final and logical development proves fatal to all other nationalities and liberties, — yea, to literature and art and science and industry, the extinction of which is the moral death of an empire, however grand and however boastful, only to be succeeded by new creations, through the fires of successive wars and hateful anarchies.

In one point, and one alone, I see the Providence which permitted the military aggrandizement to which Frederic and his successors aimed; and that is, in furnishing a barrier to the future conquests of a more barbarous people, — I mean the Russians; even as the conquests of Charlemagne presented a barrier to the future irruptions of barbarous tribes on his northern frontier. Russia — that rude, demoralized, Slavonic empire — cannot conquer Europe until it has first destroyed the political and military power of Germany. United and patriotic, Germany can keep at present the Russians at bay, and direct the stream of invasion to the East rather than the South; so that Europe will not become either Cossack or French, as Napoleon predicted. In this light the military genius and power of

Germany, which Frederic did so much to develop, may be designed for the protection of European civilization and the Protestant religion.

But I will not speculate on the aims of Providence, or the evil to be overruled for good. With my limited vision, I can only present facts and their immediate consequences. I can only deduce the moral truths which are logically to be drawn from a career of wicked ambition. These truths are a part of that moral wisdom which experience confirms, and which alone should be the guiding lesson to all statesmen and all empires. Let us pursue the right, and leave the consequences to Him who rules the fate of war, and guides the nations to the promised period when men shall beat their swords into ploughshares, and universal peace shall herald the reign of the Saviour of the world.

---

## AUTHORITIES.

THE great work of Carlyle on the Life of Frederic, which exhausts the subject; Macaulay's Essay on the Life and Times of Frederic the Great; Carlyle's Essay on Frederic; Lord Brougham on Frederic; Coxe's History of the House of Austria; Mirabeau's Histoire Sécrète de la Cour de Berlin; Œuvres de Frédéric le Grand; Ranke's Neue Bücher Preussischer Geschichte; Pöllnitz's Memoirs and Letters; Walpole's Reminiscences; Letters of Voltaire; Voltaire's Idée du Roi de Prusse; Life of Baron Trenck; Gillies' View of the Reign of Frederic II.; Thiebault's Mémoires de Frédéric le Grand; Biographe Universelle; Thronbesteigung; Holden.

# PRINCE BISMARCK.

## THE GERMAN EMPIRE.

# PRINCE BISMARCK.

―――――◆―――――

## THE GERMAN EMPIRE.

BEFORE presenting Bismarck, it will be necessary to glance at the work of those great men who prepared the way not only for him, but also for the soldier Moltke,—men who raised Prussia from the humiliation resulting from her conquest by Napoleon.

That humiliation was as complete as it was unexpected. It was even greater than that of France after the later Franco-Prussian war. Prussia was dismembered; its provinces were seized by the conqueror; its population was reduced to less than four millions; its territory was occupied by one hundred and fifty thousand French soldiers; the king himself was an exile and a fugitive from his own capital; every sort of indignity was heaped on his prostrate subjects, who were compelled to pay a war indemnity beyond their power; trade and commerce were cut off by Napoleon's Continental system; and universal poverty overspread the country, always poor, and now poorer than ever.

Prussia had no allies to rally to her sinking fortunes; she was completely isolated. Most of her fortresses were in the hands of her enemies, and the magnificent army of which she had been so proud since the days of Frederick the Great was dispersed. At the peace of Tilsit, in 1807, it looked as if the whole kingdom was about to be absorbed in the empire of Napoleon, like Bavaria and the Rhine provinces, and wiped out of the map of Europe like unfortunate Poland.

But even this did not complete the humiliation. Napoleon compelled the King of Prussia — Frederick William III. — to furnish him soldiers to fight against Russia, as if Prussia was already incorporated with his own empire and had lost her nationality. At that time France and Russia were in alliance, and Prussia had no course to adopt but submission or complete destruction; and yet Prussia refused in these evil days to join the Confederation of the Rhine, which embraced all the German States at the south and west of Austria and Prussia. Napoleon, however, was too much engrossed in his scheme of conquering Spain, to swallow up Prussia entirely, as he intended, after he should have subdued Spain. So, after all, Prussia had before her only the fortune of Ulysses in the cave of Polyphemus, — to be devoured the last.

The escape of Prussia was owing, on the one hand, to the necessity for Napoleon to withdraw his main army from Prussia in order to fight in Spain; and secondly, to the transcendent talents of a few patriots to whom the king in his distress was forced to listen. The chief of these were Stein, Hardenberg, and Scharn- horst. It was the work of Stein to reorganize the internal administration of Prussia, including the finan- cial department; that of Hardenberg to conduct the ministry of foreign affairs; and that of Scharnhorst to reorganize the military power. The two former were nobles; the latter sprung from the people, — a peasant's son; but they worked together in tolerable harmony considering the rival jealousies that at one time existed among all the high officials, with their innumerable prejudices.

Baron von Stein, born in 1757, of an old imperial knightly family from the country near Nassau, was as a youth well educated, and at the age of twenty-three entered the Prussian service under Frederick the Great, in the mining department, where he gained rapid pro- motion. In 1786 he visited England and made a careful study of her institutions, which he profoundly admired. In 1787 he became a sort of provincial governor, being director of the war and Domaine Cham- bers at Cleves and Hamm.

In 1804 Stein became Minister of Trade, having charge of excise, customs, manufactures, and trade. The whole financial administration at this time under

King Frederick William III. was in a state of great confusion, from an unnecessary number of officials who did not work harmoniously. There was too much "red tape." Stein brought order out of confusion, simplified the administration, punished corruption, increased the national credit, then at a very low ebb, and re-established the bank of Prussia on a basis that enabled it to assist the government.

But a larger field than that of finance was opened to Stein in the war of 1806. The king intrusted to him the portfolio of foreign affairs, — not willingly, but because he regarded him as the ablest man in the kingdom. Stein declined to be foreign minister unless he was entirely unshackled, and the king was obliged to yield, for the misfortunes of the country had now culminated in the disastrous defeat at Friedland. The king, however, soon quarrelled with his minister, being jealous of his commanding abilities, and unused to dictation from any source. After a brief exile at Nassau, the peace of Tilsit having proved the sagacity of his views, Stein returned to power as virtual dictator of the kingdom, with the approbation of Napoleon; but his dictatorship lasted only about a year, when he was again discharged.

During that year, 1807, Stein made his mark in Prussian history. Without dwelling on details, he effected the abolition of serfdom in Prussia, the trade in land, and municipal reforms, giving citizens self-government in place of the despotism of military bureaus. He made it his business to pay off the French war indemnity, — one hundred and fifty million francs, a great sum for Prussia to raise when dismembered and trodden in the dust under one hundred and fifty thousand French soldiers, — and to establish a new and improved administrative system. But more than all, he attempted to rouse a moral, religious, and patriotic spirit in the nation, and to inspire it anew with courage, self-confidence, and self-sacrifice. In 1808 the ministry became warlike in spite of its despair, the first glimpse of hope being the popular rising in Spain. It was during the ministry of Stein, and through his efforts, that the anti-Napoleonic revolution began.

The intense hostility of Stein to Napoleon, and his commanding abilities, led Napoleon in 1808 imperatively to demand from the King of Prussia the dismisssal of his minister; and Frederick William dared not resist. Stein did not retire, however, until after the royal edict had emancipated the serfs of Prussia, and until that other great reform was made by which the nobles lost the monopoly of office and exemption from taxation, while the citizen class gained admission to all posts, trades, and occupations. These great reforms were chiefly to be traced to Stein, although

Hardenberg and others, like Schön and Niebuhr, had a hand in them.

Stein also opened the military profession to the citizen class, which before was closed, only nobles being intrusted with command in the army. It is true that nobles still continued to form a large majority of officers, even as peasants formed the bulk of the army. But the removal of restrictions and the abolition of serfdom tended to create patriotic sentiments among all classes, on which the strength of armies in no small degree rests. In the time of Frederick the Great the army was a mere machine. It was something more when the nation in 1811 rallied to achieve their independence. Then was born the idea of nationality, — that, whatever obligations a Prussian owed to the state, Germany was greater than Prussia itself. This idea was the central principle of Stein's political system, leading ultimately to the unity of Germany as finally effected by Bismarck and Moltke. It became almost synonymous with that patriotism which sustains governments and thrones, the absence of which was the great defect of the German States before the times of Napoleon, when both princes and people lost sight of the unity of the nation in the interests of petty sovereignties.

Stein was a man of prodigious energy, practical good sense, and lofty character, but irascible, haughty, and contemptuous, and was far from being a favorite with the king and court. His great idea was the unity and independence of Germany. He thought more of German nationality than of Prussian aggrandizement. It was his aim to make his countrymen feel that they were Germans rather than Prussians, and that it was only by a union of the various German States that they could hope to shake off the French yoke, galling and humiliating beyond description.

When Stein was driven into exile at the dictation of Napoleon, with the loss of his private fortune, he was invited by the Emperor of Russia to aid him with his counsels, — and it can be scarcely doubted that in the employ of Russia he rendered immense services to Germany, and had no little influence in shaping the movements of the allies in effecting the ruin of the common despot. On this point, however, I cannot dwell.

Count, afterward Prince, Hardenberg, held to substantially the same views, and was more acceptable to the king as minister than was the austere and haughty Stein, although his morals were loose, and his abilities far inferior to those of the former. But his diplomatic talents were considerable, and his manners were agreeable, like those of Metternich, while Stein treated kings and princes as ordinary men, and dictated to them the course which was necessary to pursue. It was the

work of Hardenberg to create the peasant-proprietor-
ship of modern Prussia; but it was the previous work
of Stein to establish free trade in land, — which means
the removal of hindrances to the sale and purchase of
land, which still remains one of the abuses of England, — the ultimate effect of which was to remove
caste in land as well as caste in persons.

The great educational movement, in the deepest
depression of Prussian affairs, was headed by William
Baron von Humboldt. When Prussia lay disarmed,
dismembered, and impoverished, the University of Berlin was founded, the government contributing one
hundred and fifty thousand thalers a year; and Humboldt — the first minister of public instruction — succeeded in inducing the most eminent and learned men
in Germany to become professors in this new university. I look upon this educational movement in the
most gloomy period of German history as one of the
noblest achievements which any nation ever made in
the cause of science and literature. It took away the
sting of military ascendency, and raised men of genius
to an equality with nobles; and as the universities
were the centres of liberal sentiments and all liberal-
izing ideas, they must have exerted no small influence
on the war of liberation itself, as well as on the cause
of patriotism, which was the foundation of the future
greatness of Prussia. Students flocked from all parts

of Germany to hear lectures from accomplished and patriotic professors, who inculcated the love of father-land. Germany, though fallen into the hands of a military hero from defects in the administration of governments and armies, was not disgraced when her professors in the university were the greatest scholars of the world. They created a new empire, not of the air, as some one sneeringly remarked, but of mind, which has gone on from conquering to conquer. For more than fifty years German universities have been the centre of European thought and scholastic cul-ture, — pedantic perhaps, but original and profound.

Before proceeding to the main subject, I have to speak of one more great reform, which was the work of Scharnhorst. This was that series of measures which determined the result of the greatest military struggles of the nineteenth century, and raised Prussia to the front rank of military monarchies. It was the *levée en masse*, composed of the youth of the nation, without distinction ^f rank, instead of an army made up of peasants and serfs and commanded by their feudal masters. Scharnhorst introduced a compulsory system indeed, but it was not unequal. Every man was made to feel that he had a personal interest in defending his country, and there were no exemptions made. True, the old system of Frederick the Great was that of conscription; but from this conscription

large classes and whole districts were exempted, while
the soldiers who fought in the war of liberation were
drawn from all classes alike: hence there was no
unjust compulsion, which weakens patriotism, and en-
tails innumerable miseries.  It was impossible in the
utter exhaustion of the national finances to raise a
sufficient number of volunteers to meet the emer-
gencies of the times; therefore if Napoleon was to
be overthrown it was absolutely necessary to compel
everybody to serve in the army for a limited period.
The nation saw the necessity, and made no resistance.
Thus patriotism lent her aid, and became an overwhelming power.   The citizen soldier was no great
burden on the government, since it was bound to his
support only for a limited period, — long or short
as the exigency of the country demanded.   Hence
large armies were maintained at comparatively trifling
expense.

I need not go into the details of a system which
made Prussia a nation of patriots as well as of soldiers,
and which made Scharnhorst a great national bene-
factor, sharing with Stein the glory of a great deliver-
ance.  He did not live to see the complete triumph
of his system, matured by genius and patient study;
but his work remained to future generations, and
made Prussia invincible except to a coalition of powerful enemies.  All this was done under the eye of

Napoleon, and a dreamy middle class became an effective soldiery. So, too, did the peasants, no longer subjected to corporal punishment and other humiliations. What a great thing it was to restore dignity to a whole nation, and kindle the fires of patriotic ardor among poor and rich alike! To the credit of the king, he saw the excellence of the new system, at once adopted it, and generously rewarded its authors. Scharnhorst, the peasant's son, was made a noble, and was retained in office until he died. Stein, however, whose overshadowing greatness created jealousy, remained simply a baron, and spent his last days in retirement, — though not unhonored, or without influence, even when not occupying the great offices of state, to which no man ever had a higher claim. The king did not like him, and the king was still an absolute monarch.

Frederick William III. was by no means a great man, being jealous, timid, and vacillating; but it was in his reign that Prussia laid the foundation of her greatness as a military monarchy. It was not the king who laid this foundation, but the great men whom Providence raised up in the darkest hours of Prussia's humiliation. He did one prudent thing, however, out of timidity, when his ministers waged vigorous and offensive measures. He refused to arm against Napoleon when Prussia lay at his mercy.

This turned out to be the salvation of Prussia. A weak man's instincts proved to be wiser than the wisdom of the wise. When Napoleon's doom was sealed by his disasters in Russia, then, and not till then, did the Prussian king unite with Russia and Austria to crush the unscrupulous despot.

The condition of Prussia, then, briefly stated, when Napoleon was sent to St. Helena to meditate and die, was this: a conquering army, of which Blücher was one of its greatest generals, had been raised by the *levée en masse,* — a conscription, indeed, not of peasants alone, obliged to serve for twenty years, but of the whole nation, for three years of active service; and a series of administrative reforms had been introduced and extended to every department of the State, by which greater economy and a more complete system were inaugurated, favoritism abolished, and the finances improved so as to support the government and furnish the sinews of war; while alliances were made with great Powers who hitherto had been enemies or doubtful friends.

These alliances resulted in what is called the German Confederation, or Bund,—a strict union of all the various States for defensive purposes, and also to maintain a general system to suppress revolutionary and internal dissensions. Most of the German States entered into this Confederacy, at the head of which was Austria. It was determined in June, 1815, at Vienna, that the Confederacy should be managed by a general assembly called a Diet, the seat of which was located at Frankfort. In this Diet the various independent States, thirty-nine in number, had votes in proportion to their population, and were bound to contribute troops of one soldier to every hundred inhabitants, amounting to three hundred thousand in all, of which Austria and Prussia and Bavaria furnished more than half. This arrangement virtually gave to Austria and Prussia a preponderance in the Diet; and as the States were impoverished by the late war, and the people generally detested war, a long peace of forty years (with a short interval of a year) was secured to Germany, during which prosperity returned and the population nearly doubled. The Germans turned their swords into pruning-hooks, and all kinds of industry were developed, especially manufactures. The cities were adorned with magnificent works of art, and libraries, schools, and universities covered the land. No nation ever made a more signal progress in material prosperity than did the German States during this period of forty years, — especially Prussia, which became in addition intellectually the most cultivated country in Europe, with twenty-one thousand primary schools, and one thousand academies, or gymnasia, in which mathematics and the learned languages were taught by accomplished scholars; to say nothing of the universities, which drew students from all Christian and civilized countries in both hemispheres.

The rapid advance in learning, however, especially in the universities and the gymnasia, led to the discussion of innumerable subjects, including endless theories of government and the rights of man, by which discontent was engendered and virtue was not advanced. Strange to say, even crime increased. The universities became hot-beds of political excitement, duels, beer-drinking, private quarrels, and infidel discussion, causing great alarm to conservative governments and to peaceful citizens generally. At last the Diet began to interfere, for it claimed the general oversight of all internal affairs in the various States. An army of three hundred thousand men which obeyed the dictation of the Diet was not to be resisted; and as this Diet was controlled by Austria and Prussia, it became every year more despotic and anti-democratic. In consequence, the Press was gradually fettered, the universities were closely watched, and all revolutionary movements in cities were suppressed. Discontent and popular agitations, as usual, went hand in hand.

As early as 1818 the great reaction against all liberal sentiments in political matters had fairly set in. The king of Prussia neglected, and finally refused, to grant the constitutional government which he had promised in the day of his adversity before the battle of Waterloo; while Austria, guided by Metternich, stamped her iron heel on everything which looked like intellectual or national independence.

This memorable reaction against all progress in government, not confined to the German States but extending to Europe generally, has already been considered in previous chapters. It was the great political feature in the history of Europe for ten years after the fall of Napoleon, particularly in Austria, where hatred of all popular movements raged with exceeding bitterness, intensified by the revolutions in Spain, Italy, and Greece. The assassination of Kotzebue, the dramatic author, by a political fanatic, for his supposed complicity with the despotic schemes of the Czar, kindled popular excitement into a blazing flame, but still more fiercely incited the sovereigns of Germany to make every effort to suppress even liberty of thought.

During the period, then, when ultra-conservative principles animated the united despots of the various German States, and the Diet controlled by Metternich repressed all liberal movements, little advance was made in Prussia in the way of reforms. But a great advance was made in all questions of political economy and industrial matters. Free-trade was established in the most unlimited sense between all the states and provinces of the Confederation. All restraints were removed from the navigation of rivers; new markets were opened in every direction for the productions of industry. In 1839 the Zollverein, or Customs-Union, was established, by which a uniform scale of duties was imposed in Northern Germany on all imports and exports. But no political reforms which the king had promised were effected during the life of Frederick William III. Hardenberg, who with Stein had inaugurated liberal movements, had lost his influence, although he was retained in power until he died.

For the twenty years succeeding the confederation of the German States in 1820, constitutional freedom made little or no progress in Germany. The only advance made in Prussia was in 1823, when the Provincial Estates, or Diets, were established. These, however, were the mere shadow of representative government, since the Estates were convoked at irregular intervals, and had neither the power to initiate laws nor grant supplies. They could only express their opinions concerning changes in the laws pertaining to persons and property.

On the 7th of June, 1840, Frederick William III. of Prussia died, and was succeeded by his son Frederick William IV., a religious and patriotic king, who was compelled to make promises for some sort

of constitutional liberty, and to grant certain concessions, which although they did not mean much gave
general satisfaction. Among other things the freedom
of the Press was partially guaranteed, with certain
restrictions and the Zollverein was extended to Bruns-
wick and Hesse-Homburg. Meantime the government
entered with zeal upon the construction of railways
and the completion of the Cathedral of Cologne, which
tended to a more permanent union of the North German States. "We are not engaged here," said the
new monarch, on the inauguration of the completion
of that proudest work of mediæval art, "with the construction of an ordinary edifice; it is a work bespeak-
ing the spirit of union and concord which animates the
whole of Germany and all its persuasions, that we are
now constructing." This inauguration, amid immense
popular enthusiasm, was soon followed by the meeting of the Estates of the whole kingdom at Berlin,
which for the first time united the various Provincial
Estates in a general Diet; but its functions were
limited to questions involving a diminution of taxation.
No member was allowed to speak more than once on
any question, and the representatives of the com-
mons were only a third part of the whole assembly.
This naturally did not satisfy the nation, and peti-
tions flowed in for the abolition of the censorship
of the Press and for the publicity of debate. The

king was not prepared to make these concessions in
full, but he abolished the censorship of the Press as
to works extending to above twenty pages, and enjoined
the censors of lesser pamphlets and journals to exercise gentleness and discretion, and not erase anything
which did not strike at the monarchy.  At length, in
1847, the desire was so universal for some form of
representative government that a royal edict convoked
a General Assembly of the Estates of Prussia, arranged
in four classes, -- the nobles, the equestrian order, the
towns, and the rural districts.  The Diet consisted of
six hundred and seventy members, of which only
eighty were nobles, and was empowered to discuss all
questions pertaining to legislation ; but the initiative
of all measures was reserved to the crown..  This
National Diet assembled on the 24th of July, and was
opened by the king in person, with a noble speech,
remarkable for its elevation of tone.  He convoked
the Diet, the king said, to make himself acquainted
with the wishes and wants of his people, but not to
change the constitution, which guaranteed an absolute
monarchy.  The province of the Diet was consultative
rather than legislative.  Political and military power,
as before, remained with the king.  Still, an important
step had been taken toward representative institutions.

It was about this time, as a member of the National
Diet, that Otto Edward Leopold von Bismarck appeared

upon the political stage. It was a period of great political excitement, not only in Prussia, but throughout Europe, and also of great material prosperity. Railways had been built, the Zollverein had extended through North Germany, the universities were in their glory, and into everything fearless thinkers were casting their thoughtful eyes. Thirty-four years of peace had enriched and united the German States. The great idea of the day was political franchise. Everybody aspired to solve political problems, and wished to have a voice in deliberative assemblies. There was also an unusual agitation of religious ideas. Ronge had attempted the complete emancipation of Germany from Papal influences, and university professors threw their influence on the side of rationalism and popular liberty. On the whole there was a general tendency towards democratic ideas, which was opposed with great bitterness by the conservative parties, made up of nobles and government officials.

Bismarck arose, slowly but steadily, with the whole force of his genius, among the defenders of the conservative interests of his order and of the throne. He was then simply Herr von Bismarck, belonging to an ancient and noble but not wealthy family, whose seat was Schönhausen, where the future prince was born April 1, 1815. The youth was sent to a gymnasium in Berlin in 1830, and in 1832 to the university of

Göttingen in Hanover, where he was more distinguished for duels, drinking-parties, and general law-
lessness than for scholarship. Here he formed a
memorable friendship with a brother ~tudent, a young
American, — John Lothrop Motley, later the historian
of the Dutch Republic. Much has been written of
Bismarck's reckless and dissipated life at the university, which differed not essentially from that of other
nobles. He had a grand figure, superb health, extraordinary animal spirits, and could ride like a centaur.
He spent but three semestres at Göttingen, and then
repaired to Berlin in order to study jurisprudence
under the celebrated Savigny; but he was rarely seen
in the lecture-room. He gave no promise of the great
abilities which afterward distinguished him. Yet he
honorably passed his State examination; and as he
had chosen the law for his profession, he first served
on leaving the university as a sort of clerk in the city
police, and in 1834 was transferred to Aix-la-Chapelle,
in the administrative department of the district. In
1837 he served in the crown office at Potsdam. He
then entered for a year as a sharpshooter of the
Guards, to absolve his obligation to military service.

The next eight years, from the age of twenty-four,
he devoted to farming, hunting, carousing, and read-
ing, on one of his father's estates in Pomerania. He
was a sort of country squire, attending fairs, selling

wool, inspecting timber, handling grain, gathering rents, and sitting as a deputy in the local Diet, — the talk and scandal of the neighborhood for his demon-like rides and drinking-bouts, yet now studying all the while, especially history and even philosophy, managing the impoverished paternal estates with prudence and success, and making short visits to France and England, the languages of which countries he could speak with fluency and accuracy. In 1847 he married Johanna von Putkammer, nine years younger than himself, who proved a model wife, domestic and wise, of whom he was both proud and fond. The same year, his father having died and left him Schönhausen, he was elected a member of the Landtag, a quasi parliament of the eight united Diets of the monarchy; and his great career began.

Up to this period Bismarck was not a publicly marked man, except in an avidity for country sports and in horsemanship. He ever retained his love of the country and of country life. If proud and overbearing, he was not ostentatious. He had but few friends, but to these he was faithful. He never was popular until he had made Prussia the most powerful military State in Europe. He never sought to be loved so much as to be feared; he never allowed himself to be approached without politeness and deference. He seemed to care more for dogs than men.

Nor was he endowed with those graces of manner which marked Metternich. He remained harsh, severe, grave, proud through his whole career, from first to last, except in congenial company. What is called society he despised, with all his aristocratic tendencies and high social rank. He was born for untrammelled freedom, and was always impatient under contradiction or opposition. When he reached the summit of his power he resembled Wallenstein, the hero of the Thirty Years' War, — superstitious, self-sustained, unapproachable, inspiring awe, rarely kindling love, overshadowing by his vast abilities the monarch whom he served and ruled.

No account of the man, however, would be complete which did not recognize the corner-stone of his character, — an immovable belief in the feudalistic right of royalty to rule its subjects. Descended from an ancient family of knights and statesmen, of the most intensely aristocratic and reactionary class even in Germany, his inherited instincts and his own tremendous will, backed by a physique of colossal size and power, made effective his loyalty to the king and the monarchy, which from the first dominated and inspired him. In the National Diet of 1847, Herr von Bismarck sat for more than a month before he opened his lips; but when he did speak it became evident that he was determined to support to the utmost the power of the crown. He was *plus royaliste que le roi.* In the ordinary sense he was no orator. He hesitated, he coughed, he sought for words; his voice, in spite of his herculean frame, was feeble. But sturdy in his loyalty, although inexperienced in parliamentary usage, he offered a bold front to the liberalism which he saw to be dangerous to his sovereign's throne. Like Oliver Cromwell in Parliament, he gained daily in power, while, unlike the English statesman, he was opposed to the popular side, and held up the monarchy after the fashion of Strafford. From that time, and in fact until 1866 when he conquered Austria, Bismarck was very unpopular; and as he rose in power he became the most bitterly hated man in Prussia, — which hatred he returned with arrogant contempt. He consistently opposed all reforms, even the emancipation of the Jews, which won him the favor of the monarch.

When the revolution of 1848 broke out, which hurled Louis Philippe from the French throne, its flames reached every continental State except Russia. Metternich, who had been all powerful in Austria for forty years, was obliged to flee, as well as the imperial family itself. All the Germanic States were now promised liberal constitutions by the fallen or dismayed princes. In Prussia affairs were critical, and the reformers were sanguine of triumph. Berlin was agitated by mobs to the verge of anarchy. The king, seriously alarmed, now promised the boon which he had thus far withheld, and summoned the Second United Diet to pave the way for a constituent assembly. In this constituent assembly Bismarck scorned to sit. For six months it sat squabbling and fighting, but accomplishing nothing. At last Bismarck found it expedient to enter the new parliament as a deputy, and again vigorously upheld the absolute power of the crown. He did, indeed, accept the principle of constitutional government, but, as he frankly said, against his will, and only as a new power in the hands of the monarch to restrain popular agitation and maintain order. Through his influence the king refused the imperial crown offered by the Frankfort parliament, because he conceived that the parliament had no right to give it, that its acceptance would be a recognition of national instead of royal sovereignty, and that it would be followed probably by civil war. As time went on he became more and more the leader of the conservatives. I need not enumerate the subjects which came up for discussion in the new Prussian parliament, in which Bismarck exhibited with more force than eloquence his loyalty to the crown, and a conservatism which was branded by the liberals as mediæval. But his originality, his boldness, his fearlessness, his rugged earnestness, his wit and humor,

his biting sarcasm, his fertility of resources, his knowledge of men and affairs, and his devoted patriotism,
marked him out for promotion.

In 1851 Bismarck was sent as first secretary of the
Prussian embassy to the Diet of the various German
States, convened at Frankfort, in which Austria held
a predominating influence. It was not a parliament,
but an administrative council of the Germanic Confederation founded by the Congress of Vienna in 1815.
It made no laws, and its sittings were secret. It was
a body which represented the League of Sovereigns,
and was composed of only seventeen delegates, —
its main function being to suppress all liberal movements in the various German States; like the Congress
of Vienna itself. The Diet of Frankfort was pretentious, but practically impotent, and was the laughing-
stock of Europe. It was full of jealousies and
intrigues. It was a mere diplomatic conference. As
Austria and Prussia controlled it, things went well
enough when these two Powers were agreed; but they
did not often agree. There was a perpetual rivalry
between them, and an unextinguishable jealousy.

There were many sneers at the appointment of a man
to this diplomatic post whose manners were brusque
and overbearing, and who had spent the most of his
time, after leaving the university, among horses, cattle,
and dogs; who was only a lieutenant of militia, with a

single decoration, and who was unacquainted with
what is called diplomacy. But the king knew his
man, and the man was conscious of his powers.

Bismarck found life at Frankfort intolerably dull.
He had a contempt for his diplomatic associates generally, and made fun of them to his few intimate friends.
He took them in almost at a glance, for he had an in-
tuitive knowledge of character; he weighed them in his
balance, and found them wanting. In a letter to his
wife he writes: "Nothing but miserable trifles do
these people trouble themselves about. They strike
me as infinitely more ridiculous with their important
ponderosity concerning the gathered rags of gossip,
than even a member of the Second Chamber of Berlin
in the full consciousness of his dignity. . . . The
men of the minor States are mostly mere caricatures
of periwig diplomatists, who at once put on their
official visage if I merely beg of them a light to my
cigar."

His extraordinary merits were however soon apparent to the king, and even to his chief, old General
Rochow, who was soon transferred to St. Petersburg
to make way for the secretary. The king's brother
William, Prince of Prussia, when at Frankfort, was
much impressed by the young Prussian envoy to the
Bund, and there was laid the foundation of the friendship between the future soldier-king and the future

chancellor, between whom there always existed a warm confidence and esteem. Soon after, Bismarck made the acquaintance of Metternich, who had ruled for so long a time both the Diet and the Empire. The old statesman, now retired, invited the young diplomatist to his castle at Johannisberg. They had different aims, but similar sympathies. The Austrian statesman sought to preserve the existing state of things; the Prussian, to make his country dominant over Germany. Both were aristocrats, and both were conservative; but Metternich was as bland and polished as Bismarck was rough and brusque.

Nothing escaped the watchful eye of Bismarck at Frankfort as the ambassador of Prussia. He took note of everything, both great and small, and communicated it to Berlin as if he were a newspaper correspondent. In everything he showed his sympathy with absolutism, and hence recommended renewed shackles on the Press and on the universities, — at that time the hotbed of revolutionary ideas. His central aim and constant thought was the ascendency of Prussia, — first in royal strength at home, then throughout Germany as the rival of Austria. Bismarck was not only a keen observer, but he soon learned to disguise his thoughts. Nobody could read him. He was frank when his opponents were full of lies, knowing that he would not be believed. He became a perfect master of the art of deception. No one was a match for him in statecraft. Even Prince Gortschakoff became his dupe. By his tact he kept Prussia from being entangled by the usurpation of Napoleon III., and by the Crimean war. He saw into the character of the French emperor, and discovered that he was shallow, and not to be feared. At Frankfort Bismarck had many opportunities of seeing distinguished men of all nations; he took their gauge, and penetrated the designs of cabinets. He counselled his master to conciliate Napoleon, though regarding him as an upstart; and he sought the friendship of France in order to eclipse the star of Austria, whom it was necessary to humble before Prussia could rise. In his whole diplomatic career at Frankfort it was Bismarck's aim to contravene the designs of Austria, having in view the aggrandizement of Prussia as the true head and centre of German nationality. He therefore did all he could to prevent Austria from being assisted in her war with Italy, and rejoiced in her misfortunes. In the mean time he made frequent short visits to Holland, Denmark, Italy, and Hungary, acquired the languages of these countries, and made himself familiar with their people and institutions, besides shrewdly studying the characters, manners, and diplomatic modes of the governing classes of European nations at large. Cool, untiring, self-possessed, he was storing up information and experience.

At the end of eight years, in 1859, Bismarck was transferred to St. Petersburg as the Prussian ambassador to Alexander II. He was then forty-three years of age, and was known as the sworn foe of Austria. His free-and-easy but haughty manners were a great contrast to those of his stiff, buttoned-up, and pretentious predecessors; and he became a great favorite in Russian court circles. The comparatively small salary he received, — less than twenty thousand dollars, with a house, — would not allow him to give expensive entertainments, or to run races in prodigality with the representatives of England, France, or even Austria, who received nearly fifty thousand dollars. But no parties were more sought or more highly appreciated than those which his sensible and unpretending wife gave in the high society in which they moved. With the empress dowager he was an especial favorite, and was just the sort of man whom the autocrat of all the Russias would naturally like, especially for his love of hunting, and his success in shooting deer and bears. He did not go to grand parties any more than he could help, despising their ostentation and frivolity, and always feeling the worse for them.

On the 2d of January, 1861, Frederick William IV., who had for some time been insane, died, and was succeeded by the Prince Regent William I., already in his sixty-fifth year, every inch a soldier and nothing else. Bismarck was soon summoned to the councils of his sovereign at Berlin, who was perplexed and annoyed by the Liberal party, which had the ascendency in the lower Chamber of the general Diet. Office was pressed upon Bismarck, but before he accepted it he wished to study Napoleon and French affairs more closely, and was therefore sent as ambassador to Paris in 1862. He made that year a brief visit to London, Disraeli being then the premier, who smiled at his schemes for the regeneration of Germany. It was while journeying amid the Pyrenees that Bismarck was again summoned to Berlin, the lower Chamber having ridden rough-shod over his Majesty's plans for army reform. The king invested him with the great office of President of the Ministry, his abilities being universally recognized.

It was now Bismarck's mission to break the will of the Prussian parliament, and to thrust Austria out of the Germanic body. He considered only the end in view, caring nothing for the means: he had no scruples. It was his religion to raise Prussia to the same ascendency that Austria had held under Metternich. He had a master whose will and ambition were equal to his own, yet whose support he was sure of in carrying out his grand designs. He was now a second Richelieu, to whom the aggrandizement of the mon-

archy which he served and the welfare of Fatherland
were but-convertible terms. He soon came into bitter
conflict, not with nobles, but with progressive liberals
in the Chamber, who detested him and feared him, but
to whom he did not condescend to reveal his plans, —
bearing obloquy with placidity in the greatness of the
end he had in view. He was a self-sustained, haughty,
unapproachable man of power, except among the few
friends whom he honored as boon companions, without
ever losing his discretion, — wearing a mask with apparent frankness, and showing real frankness in matters
which did not concern secrets of state, especially on
the subjects of education and religion. Like his master, he was more a Calvinist than a Lutheran. He
openly avowed his dependence on Almighty God, and
on him alone, as the hope of nations. In this respect
we trace a resemblance to Oliver Cromwell rather than
to Frederick the Great. Bismarck was a compound
of both, in his patriotism and his unscrupulousness.

The first thing that King William and his minister
did was to double the army. But this vast increase
of military strength seemed unnecessary to the Liberal
party, and the requisite increase of taxes to support
it was unpopular. Hence Bismarck was brought in
conflict with the lower Chamber, which represented
the middle classes. He dared not tell his secret
schemes without imperilling their success, which led

to grave misunderstandings. For four years the conflict raged between the crown and the parliament, both
the king and Bismarck being inflexible; and the lower
House was equally obstinate in refusing to grant the
large military supplies demanded. At last Bismarck
dissolved the Chambers, and the king declared that
as the Three Estates could not agree, he should continue to do his duty by Prussia without regard to
"these pieces of paper called constitutions." The next
four sessions of the Chamber were closed in the same
manner. Bismarck admitted that he was acting un-
constitutionally, but claimed the urgency of public
necessity. In the public debates he was cool, sar-
castic, and contemptuous. The Press took up the
fight, and the Press was promptly muzzled. Bismarck was denounced as a Catiline, a Strafford, a
Polignac; but he retained a provoking serenity, and
quietly prepared for war, — since war, he foresaw,
was sooner or later inevitable. "Nothing can solve
the question," said he, "but blood and iron."

At last an event occurred which showed his hand.
In November, 1863, Frederick VII., the king of Denmark, died. By his death the Schleswig-Holstein question again burst upon distracted Europe, — Who was
to reign over the two Danish provinces? The king
of Denmark, as Duke of Schleswig and Holstein, had
been represented in the Germanic Diet. By the treaty

of London, in 1852, he had undertaken not to incorporate the duchies with the rest of his monarchy, allowing them to retain their traditional autonomy. In 1863, shortly before his death, Frederick VII. by a decree dissolved this autonomy, and virtually incorporated Schleswig, which was only partly German, with the Danish monarchy, leaving the wholly German Holstein as before. Bismarck protested against this violation of treaty obligations. The Danish parliament nevertheless passed a law which incorporated the province with Denmark; and Charles IX., the new monarch, confirmed the law.

But a new claimant to the duchies now appeared in the person of Frederick of Augustenburg, a German prince; and the Prussian Chamber advocated his claims, as did the Diet itself; but the throne held its opinion in reserve. Bismarck contrived (by what diplomatic tricks and promises it is difficult to say) to induce Austria to join with Prussia in seizing the provinces in question and in dividing the spoil between them. As these two Powers controlled the Diet at Frankfort, it was easy to carry out the programme. An Austro-Prussian army accordingly invaded Schleswig-Holstein, and to the scandal of all Europe drove the Danish defenders to the wall. It was regarded in the same light as the seizure of Silesia by Frederick the Great, — a high-handed and un-

scrupulous violation of justice and right.    England
was particularly indignant, and uttered loud protests.
So did the lesser States of Germany, jealous of the
aggrandizement of Prussia.    Even the Prussian Chamber refused to grant the money for such an enterprise.

But Bismarck laughed in his sleeve.    This archdiplomatist had his reasons, which he did not care
to explain.    He had in view the weakening of the
power of the Diet, and a quarrel with Austria.    True,
he had embraced Austria, but after the fashion of a
bear.    He knew that Austria and Prussia would
wrangle about the division of the spoil, which would
lead to misunderstandings, and thus furnish the pretext for a war, which he felt to be necessary before
Prussia could be aggrandized and German unity be
effected, with Prussia at its head, — the two great
objects of his life.    His policy was marvellously astute; but he kept his own counsels, and continued
to hug his secret enemy.

On the 30th of October 1864, the Treaty of Vienna
was signed, by which it was settled that the king
of Denmark should surrender Schleswig-Holstein and
Lauenburg to Austria and Prussia, and he bound himself to submit to what their majesties might think fit
as to the disposition of these three duchies.    Probably both parties sought an occasion to quarrel, since
their commissioners had received opposite instructions,

—the Austrians defending the claims of Frederick of Augustenburg, as generally desired in Germany, and the Prussians now opposing them. Prussia demanded the expulsion of the pretender; to which Austria said no. Prussia further sounded Austria as to the annexation of the duchies to herself, to which Austria consented on condition of receiving an equivalent of some province in Silesia. "What!" thought Bismarck, angrily, "give you back part of what was won for Prussia by Frederick the Great? Never!" Affairs had a gloomy look; but war was averted for a while by the Convention of Gastein, by which the possession of Schleswig was assigned to Prussia, and Holstein to Austria; and further, in consideration of two and a half millions of dollars, the Emperor Francis Joseph ceded to King William all his rights of co-proprietorship in the Duchy of Lauenburg.

But the Chamber of Berlin boldly declared this transaction to be null and void, since the country had not been asked to ratify the treaty. It must be borne in mind that the conflict was still going on between Bismarck, as the defender of the absolute sovereignty of the king, and the liberal and progressive members of the Chamber, who wanted a freer and more democratic constitution. Opposed, then, by the Chamber, Bismarck dissolved it, and coolly reminded his enemies that the Chamber had nothing to do with politics, —

only with commercial affairs and matters connected with taxation. This was the period of his greatest unpopularity, since his policy and ultimate designs were not comprehended. So great was the popular detestation in which he was held that a fanatic tried to kill him in the street, but only succeeded in wounding him slightly.

In the mean time Austria fomented disaffection in the provinces which Prussia had acquired, and Bismarck resolved to cut the knot by the sword. Prussian troops marched to the frontier, and Austria on her part also prepared for war. It is difficult to see that a real *casus belli* existed. We only know that both parties wanted to fight, whatever were their excuses and pretensions; and both parties sought the friendship of Russia and France, especially by holding out delusive hopes to Napoleon of accession of territory. They succeeded in inducing both Russia and France to remain neutral, — mere spectators of the approaching contest, which was purely a German affair. It was the first care of Prussia to prevent the military union of her foes in North Germany with her foes in the south, — which was effected in part by the diplomatic genius of Bismarck, and in part by occupying the capitals of Hanover, Saxony, and Hesse-Cassel with Prussian troops, in a very summary way.

The encounter now began in earnest between Prus-

sia and Austria for the prize of ascendency. Both
parties were confident of success, — Austria as the
larger State, with proud traditions, triumphant over
rebellious Italy; and Prussia, with its enlarged military organization and the new breech-loading needle-
gun.

Count von Moltke at this time came prominently on
the European stage as the greatest strategist since Napoleon. He was chief of staff to the king, who was
commander-in-chief. He set his wonderful machinery
in harmonious action, and from his office in Berlin
moved his military pawns by touch of electric wire.
Three great armies were soon centralized in Bo-
hemia, — one of three corps, comprising one hundred
thousand men, led by Prince Charles, the king's
nephew; the second, of four corps, of one hundred
and sixteen thousand men, commanded by the crown
prince, the king's son; and the third, of forty thousand, led by General von Bittenfield. "March sep-
arately; strike together," were the orders of Moltke.
Vainly did the Austrians attempt to crush these
armies in detail before they should combine at the
appointed place. On they came, with mathematical
accuracy, until two of the armies reached Gitschin, the
objective point, where they were joined by the king, by
Moltke, by Bismarck, and by General von Roon, the war
minister. On the 2d of June, 1866, they were oppo-

site Königgrätz (or Sadowa, as the Austrians called it), where the Austrians were marshalled. On the 3d of July the battle began; and the scales hung pretty evenly until, at the expected hour, the crown prince — "our Fritz," as the people affectionately called him after this, later the Emperor Frederick William — made his appearance on the field with his army. Assailed on both flanks and pressed in the centre, the Austrians first began to slacken fire, then to waver, then to give way under the terrific concentrated fire of the needle-guns, then to retreat into ignominious flight. The contending forces were about equal; but science and the needle-gun won the day, and changed the whole aspect of modern warfare. The battle of Königgrätz settled this point, — that success in war depends more on good powder and improved weapons than on personal bravery or even masterly evolutions. Other things being equal, victory is almost certain to be on the side of the combatants who have the best weapons. The Prussians won the day of Königgrätz by their breech-loading guns, although much was due to their superior organization and superior strategy.

That famous battle virtually ended the Austro-Prussian campaign, which lasted only about seven weeks. It was one of those "decisive battles" that made Prussia the ascendent power in Germany, and destroyed the prestige of Austria. It added territory to Prussia equal to one quarter of the whole kingdom, and increased her population by four and a half millions of people. At a single bound, Prussia became a first-class military State.

The Prussian people were almost frantic with joy; and Bismarck, from being the most unpopular man in the nation, became instantly a national idol. His marvellous diplomacy, by which Austria was driven to the battlefield, was now seen and universally acknowledged. He obtained fame, decorations, and increased power. A grateful nation granted to him four hundred thousand thalers, with which he bought the estate of Varzin. General von Moltke received three hundred thousand thalers and immense military prestige. The war minister, Von Roon, also received three hundred thousand thalers. These three stood out as the three most prominent men of the nation, next to the royal family.

Never was so short a war so pregnant with important consequences. It consolidated the German Confederation under Prussian dominance. By weakening Austria it led to the national unity of Italy, and secured free government to the whole Austrian empire, since that government could no longer refuse the demands of Hungary. Above all, " it shattered the fabric of Ultramontanism which had been built up by the concordat of 1853."

It was the expectation of Napoleon III. that Austria would win in this war; but the loss of the Austrians was four to one, besides her humiliation, condemned as she was to pay a war indemnity, with the loss also of the provinces of Schleswig-Holstein, Hanover, Hesse-Cassel, Nassau, and Frankfort. But Bismarck did not push Austria to the wall, since he did not wish to make her an irreconcilable enemy. He left open a door for future and permanent peace. He did not desire to ruin his foe, but simply to acquire the lead in German politics and exclude Austria from the Germanic Confederation. Napoleon, disappointed and furious, blustered, and threatened war unless he too could come in for a share of the plunder, to which he had no real claim. Bismarck calmly replied, " Well, then, let there. be war," knowing full well that France was not prepared. Napoleon consulted his marshals. "Are we prepared," asked he, "to fight all Germany?" "Certainly not," replied the marshals, "until our whole army, like that of Prussia, is supplied with a breech-loader; until our drill is modified to suit the new weapon; until our fortresses are in a perfect state of preparedness, and until we create a mobile and efficient national reserve."

When Carlyle heard the news of the great victories of Prussia, he wrote to a friend, " Germany is to stand on her feet henceforth, and face all manner of

Napoleons and hungry, sponging dogs, with clear steel in her hand and an honest purpose in her heart. This seems to me the best news we or Europe have heard for the last forty years or more."

The triumphal return of the Prussian troops to Berlin was followed on the 24th of February, 1867, by the opening of the first North German parliament, — three hundred deputies chosen from the various allied States by universal suffrage. Twenty-two States north of the Main formed themselves into a perpetual league for the protection of the Union and its institutions. Legislative power was to be invested in two bodies, — the Reichstag, representing the people; and the Bundesrath, composed of delegates from the allied governments, the perpetual presidency of which was invested in the king of Prussia. He was also acknowledged as the commander-in-chief of the united armies; and the standing army, on a peace footing, was fixed at one per cent of all the inhabitants. This constitution was drawn by Bismarck himself, not unwilling, under the unquestioned supremacy of his monarch, to utilize the spirit of the times, and admit the people to a recognized support of the crown.

Thus Germany at last acquired a liberal constitution, though not so free and broad as that of England. The absolute control of the army and navy, the power to make treaties and declare peace and war, the appointment of all the great officers of state, and the control of education and other great interests still remained with the king. The functions of the lower House seemed to be mostly confined to furnishing the sinews of war and government, — the granting of money and regulation of taxes. Meanwhile secret treaties of alliance were concluded with the southern States of Germany, offensive and defensive, in case of war, — another stroke of diplomatic ability on the part of Bismarck; for the intrigues of Napoleon had been incessant to separate the southern from the northern States, — in other words, to divide Germany, which the French emperor was sanguine he could do. With a divided Germany, he believed that he was more than a match for the king of Prussia, as soon as his military preparations should be made. Could he convert these States into allies, he was ready for war. He was intent upon securing for France territorial enlargements equal to those of Prussia. He could no longer expect anything on the Rhine, and he turned his eyes to Belgium.

The war cloud arose on the political horizon in 1867, when Napoleon sought to purchase from the king of Holland the Duchy of Luxemburg, which was a personal fief of his kingdom, though it was inhabited by Germans, and which made him a member of the Germanic Confederation if he chose to join it. In the time of Napoleon I. Luxemburg was defended by one of the strongest fortresses in Europe, garrisoned by Prussian troops; it was therefore a menace to France on her northeastern frontier. As Napoleon III. promised a very big sum of money for this duchy, with a general protectorate of Holland in case of Prussian aggressions, the king of Holland was disposed to listen to the proposal of the French emperor; but when it was discovered that an alliance of the southern States had been made with the northern States of Germany, which made Prussia the mistress of Germany, the king of Holland became alarmed, and declined the French proposals. The chagrin of the emperor and the wrath of the French nation became unbounded. Again they had been foiled by the archdiplomatist of Prussia.

All this was precisely what Bismarck wanted. Confident of the power of Prussia, he did all he could to drive the French nation to frenzy. He worked on a vainglorious, excitable, and proud people, at the height of their imperial power. Napoleon was irresolute, although it appeared to him that war with Prussia was the only way to recover his prestige from the mistakes of the Mexican expedition. But Mexico had absorbed the marrow of the French army, and the emperor was not quite ready for war. He must find some pretence for abandoning his designs on Luxem-

burg, any attempt to seize which would be a plain
*casus belli.* Both parties were anxious to avoid the
initiative of a war which might shake Europe to its
centre. Both parties pretended peace; but both desired
war.

Napoleon, a man fertile in resources, in order to
avoid immediate hostilities looked about for some way
to avoid what he knew was premature; so he proposed submitting the case to arbitration, and the
Powers applied themselves to extinguish the gathering flames. The conference — composed of representatives of England, France, Russia, Austria, Prussia,
Holland, and Belgium — met in London; and the
result of it was that Prussia agreed to withdraw her
garrison from Luxemburg and to dismantle the fortress, while the duchy was to continue to be a member
of the German Zollverein, or Customs Union. King
William was willing to make this concession to the
cause of humanity; and his minister, rather than go
against the common sentiment of Europe, reluctantly
conceded this point, which, after all, was not of para-
mount importance. Thus was war prevented for a
time, although everybody knew that it was inevitable,
sooner or later.

The next three years Bismarck devoted himself to
diplomatic intrigues in order to cement the union of the
German States, — for the Luxemburg treaty was well

known to be a mere truce, — and Napoleon did the same to weaken the union. In the mean time King William accepted an invitation of Napoleon to visit Paris at the time of the Great Exposition ; and thither he went, accompanied by Counts Bismarck and Moltke. The party was soon after joined by the Czar, accompanied by Prince Gortschakoff, who had the reputation of being the ablest diplomatist in Europe, next to Bismarck. The meeting was a sort of carnival of peace, hollow and pretentious, with fêtes and banquets and military displays innumerable. The Prussian minister amused himself by feeling the national pulse, while Moltke took long walks to observe the fortifications of Paris. When his royal guests had left, Napoleon travelled to Salzburg to meet the Austrian emperor, ostensibly to condole with him for the unfortunate fate of Maximilian in Mexico, but really to interchange political ideas. Bismarck was not deceived, and openly maintained that the military and commercial interests of north and south Germany were identical.

In April, 1868, the Customs Parliament assembled in Berlin, as the first representative body of the entire nation that had as yet met. Though convoked to discuss tobacco and cotton, the real object was to pave the way for " the consummation of the national destinies."

Bismarck meanwhile conciliated Hanover, whose sovereign, King George, had been dethroned, by giving him a large personal indemnity, and by granting home rule to what was now a mere province of Prussia. In Berlin he resisted in the Reichstag the constitutional encroachments which the Liberal party aimed at, — ever an autocrat rather than minister, having no faith in governmental responsibility to parliament. Only one master he served, and that was the king, as Richelieu served Louis XIII. Nor would he hear of a divided ministry; affairs were too complicated to permit him to be encumbered by colleagues. He maintained that public affairs demanded quickness, energy, and unity of action; and it was certainly fortunate for Germany in the present crisis that the foreign policy was in the hands of a single man, and that man so able, decided, and astute as Bismarck.

All the while secret preparations for war went on in both Prussia and France. French spies overran the Rhineland, and German draughtsmen were busy in the cities and plains of Alsace-Lorraine. France had at last armed her soldiers with the breech-loading chassepot gun, by many thought to be superior to the needle-gun; and she had in addition secretly constructed a terrible and mysterious engine of war called *mitrailleuse,* — a combination of gun-barrels fired by mechanism. These were to effect great results. On paper, four hundred and fifty thousand men were ready to rush as an irresistible avalanche on the Rhine provinces. To the distant observer it seemed that France would gain an easy victory, and once again occupy Berlin. Besides her supposed military forces, she still had a great military prestige. Prussia had done nothing of signal importance for forty years except to fight the duel with Austria; but France had done the same, and had signally conquered at Solferino. Yet during forty years Prussia had been organizing her armies on the plan which Scharnhorst had furnished, and had four hundred and fifty thousand men under arms, — not on paper, but really ready for the field, including a superb cavalry force. The combat was to be one of material forces, guided by science.

I have said that only a pretext was needed to begin hostilities. This pretext on the part of the French was that their ambassador to Berlin, Benedetti, was reported to have been insulted by the king. He was not insulted. The king simply refused to have further parley with an arrogant ambassador, and referred him to his government, — which was the proper thing to do. On this bit of scandal the French politicians — the people who led the masses — lashed themselves into fury, and demanded immediate war.

Napoleon could not resist the popular pressure, and war was proclaimed. The arrogant demand of Napoleon, through his ambassador Benedetti, that the king of Prussia should agree never to permit his relative, Prince Leopold of Hohenzollern, to accept the vacant throne of Spain, to which he had been elected by the provisional government of that country, was the occasion of King William's curt reception of the French envoy; for this was an insulting demand, not to be endured. It was no affair of Napoleon, especially since the prince had already declined the throne at the request of the king of Prussia, as the head of the Hohenzollern family. But the French nation generally, the Catholic Church party working through the Empress Eugènie, and, above all, the excitable Parisians, goaded by the orators and the Press, saw the possibility of an extension òf the Roman empire of Charles V., under the control of Prussia ; and Napoleon was driven to the fatal course, first, of making the absurd demand, and then — in spite of a wholesome irresolution, born of his ignorance concerning his own military forces — of resenting its declinature with war.

In two weeks the German forces were mobilized, and the colossal organization, in three great armies, all directed by Moltke as chief of staff to the commander-in-chief, the still vigorous old man who ruled and governed at Berlin, were on their way to the seat of war. At Mayence the king in person, on the 2d of August, 1870, assumed command of the united German armies; and in one month from that date France was prostrate at his feet.

It would be interesting to detail the familiar story; but my limits will not permit. I can only say that the three armies of the German forces, each embracing several corps, were, one under the command of General Steinmetz, another under Prince Frederic Charles, and the third under the crown prince, — and all under the orders of Moltke, who represented the king. The crown prince, on the extreme left, struck the first blow at Weissenburg, on the 4th of August; and on the 6th he assaulted McMahon at Worth, and drove back his scattered forces, — partly on Chalons, and partly on Strasburg; while Steinmetz, commanding the right wing, nearly annihilated Frossard's corps at Spicheren. It was now the aim of the French under Bazaine, who commanded two hundred and fifty thousand men near Metz, to join McMahon's defeated forces. This was frustrated by Moltke in the bloody battle of Gravelotte, compelling Bazaine to retire within the lines of Metz, the strongest fortress in France, which was at once surrounded by Prince Charles. Meanwhile the crown prince continued the pursuit of McMahon, who had found it impossible to effect a junction with Bazaine.

At Sedan the armies met; but as the Germans were more than twice the number of the French, and had completely surrounded them, the struggle was useless, —and the French, with the emperor himself, were compelled to surrender as prisoners of war. Thus fell Napoleon's empire.

After the battle of Sedan, one of the decisive battles of history, the Germans advanced rapidly to Paris, and King William took up his quarters at Versailles, with his staff and his councillor Bismarck, who had attended him day by day through the whole campaign, and conducted the negotiations of the surrender. Paris, defended by strong fortifications, resolved to sustain a siege rather than yield, hoping that something might yet turn up by which the besieged garrison should be relieved, — a forlorn hope, as Paris was surrounded, especially on the fall of Metz, by nearly half a million of the best soldiers in the world. Yet that memorable siege lasted five months, and Paris did not yield until reduced by extreme famine; and perhaps it might have held out much longer if it could have been provisioned. But this was not to be. The Germans took the city as Alaric had taken Rome, without much waste of blood.

The conquerors were now inexorable, and demanded a war indemnity of five milliards of francs, and the cession of Metz and the two provinces of Alsace-Lorraine (which Louis XIV. had formerly wrested away), including Strasburg. Eloquently but vainly did old Thiers plead for better terms; but he pleaded with men as hard as iron, who exacted, however, no more than Napoleon III. would have done had the fortune of war enabled him to reach Berlin as the conqueror. War is hard under any circumstances, but never was national humiliation more complete than when the Prussian flag floated over the Arc de Triomphe, and Prussian soldiers defiled beneath it.

Nothing was now left for the aged Prussian king but to put upon his head the imperial crown of Germany, for all the German States were finally united under him. The scene took place at Versailles in the Hall of Mirrors, in probably the proudest palace ever erected since the days of Nebuchadnezzar. Surrounded by princes and generals, Chancellor Bismarck read aloud the Proclamation of the Empire, and the new German emperor gave thanks to God. It was a fitting sequence to the greatest military success since Napoleon crushed the German armies at Jena and Austerlitz. The tables at last were turned, and the heavy, phlegmatic, intelligent Teutons triumphed over the warlike and passionate Celts. So much for the genius of the greatest general and the greatest diplomatist that Europe had known for half a century.

Bismarck's rewards for his great services were mag-

nificent, quite equal to those of Wellington or Marl-
borough.   He received another valuable estate, this
time from his sovereign, which gift made him one of
the greatest landed proprietors of Prussia; he was
created a Prince; he was decorated with the principal
orders of Europe; he had augmented power as chancellor of confederated Germany; he was virtual dictator of his country, which he absolutely ruled in the
name of a wearied old man passed seventy years of age.

But the minister's labors and vexations do not
end with the Franco-German war.   During the years
that immediately follow, he is still one of the hard-
est-worked men in Europe.   He receives one thousand letters and telegrams a day.   He has to manage
an unpractical legislative assembly, clamorous for
new privileges, and attend to the complicated affairs
of a great empire, and direct his diplomatic agents in
every country of Europe.   He finds that the sanctum
of a one-man power is not a bed of roses.   Sometimes
he seeks rest and recreation on one of his estates, but
labors and public duties follow him wherever he goes.
He is too busy and preoccupied even for pleasure,
unless he is hunting boars and stags.   He seems to
care but little for art of any kind, except music; he
never has visited the Museum of Berlin but once in
his life; he never goes to the theatre.   He appears
as little as possible in the streets, but when recognized

he is stared at as a wonder.  He lives hospitably but plainly, and in a palace with few ornaments or luxuries.  He enshrouds himself in mystery, but not in gloom.  Few dare approach him, for his manners are brusque and rough, and he is feared more even than he is honored.  His aspect is stern and haughty, except when he occasionally unbends.  In his family he is simple, frank, and domestic; but in public he is the cold and imperative dictator.  Even the royal family are uncomfortable in his commanding and majestic presence; everybody stands in awe of him but his wife and children.  He caresses only his dogs.  He eats but once a day, but his meal is enough for five men; he drinks a quart of beer or wine without taking the cup from his mouth; he smokes incessantly, generally a long Turkish pipe.  He sleeps irregularly, disturbed by thoughts which fill his troubled brain.  Honored is the man who is invited to his table, even if he be the ambassador of a king; for at table the host is frank and courteous, and not overbearing like a literary dictator  He is well read in history, but not in art or science or poetry.  His stories are admirable when he is in convivial mood; all sit around him in silent admiration, for no one dares more than suggest the topic, — he does all the talking himself.  Bayard Taylor, when United States minister at Berlin, was amazed and confounded by his freedom of speech and apparent candor. He is frank in matters he does not care to conceal, and simple as a child when not disputed or withstood, but when opposed fierce as a lion, — a spoiled man of success, yet not intoxicated with power. Haughty and irritable perhaps, but never vain like a French statesman in office, — a Webster rather than a Thiers.

Such is the man who has ruled the German empire with an iron hand for twenty years or more, — the most remarkable man of power known to history for seventy-five years; immortal like Cavour, and for his services even more than his abilities. He has raised Prussia to the front rank among nations, and created German unity. He has quietly effected more than Richelieu ever aspired to perform; for Richelieu sought only to build up a great throne, while Bismarck has united a great nation in patriotic devotion to Fatherland, which so far as we can see, is as invincible as it is enlightened, — enlightened in everything except in democratic ideas.

I will not dwell on the career and character of Prince Bismarck after the Franco-Prussian war. He has not since been identified with any great national movements which command universal interest. His labors have been chiefly confined to German affairs, — quarrels with the Reichstag, settlement of difficulties with the various States of the Germanic Confederation, the consolidation of the internal affairs of the empire while he carried on diplomatic relations with other great Powers, efforts to gain the good-will of Russia and secure the general peace of Europe. These, and a multitude of other questions too recent to be called historical, he has dealt with, in all of which his autocratic sympathies called out the censures of the advocates of greater liberty, and diminished his popularity. For twenty years his will was the law of the German Confederation; though bitterly opposed at times by the Liberals, he was always sustained by his imperial master, who threw the burdens of State on his herculean shoulders, sometimes too great to bear with placidity. His foreign policy has been less severely criticised than his domestic, which was alternate success and failure.

The war which he waged with the spiritual power was perhaps the most important event of his administration, and in which he had not altogether his own way, underrating, as is natural to such a man, spiritual forces as compared with material. In his memorable quarrel with Rome he appeared to the least advantage, — at first rigid, severe, and arbitrary with the Catholic clergy, even to persecution, driving away the Jesuits (1872), shutting up schools and churches, imprisoning and fining ecclesiastical dignitaries, intolerant in some cases as the Inquisition itself. One quarter of the people of the empire are Catholics, yet he sternly sought to suppress their religious rights and liberties as they regarded them, thinking he could control them by material penalties,—such as taking away their support, and shutting them up in prison,—forgetting that conscientious Christians, whether Catholics or Protestants, will in matters of religion defy the mightiest rulers. No doubt the policy of the Catholics of Germany was extremely irritating to a despotic ruler who would exalt the temporal over the spiritual power; and equally true was it that the Pope himself was unyielding in regard to the liberties of his church, demanding everything and giving back nothing, in accordance with the uniform traditions of Papal domination. The Catholics, the world over, look upon the education of their children as a thing to be superintended by their own religious teachers,—as their inalienable right and imperative duty; and any State interference with this right and this duty they regard as religious persecution, to which they will never submit without hostility and relentless defiance. Bismarck felt that to concede to the demands which the Catholic clergy ever have made in respect to religious privileges was to "go to Canossa,"—where Henry IV. Emperor of Germany, in 1077, humiliated himself before Pope Gregory VII. in order to gain absolution. The long-sighted and experienced Thiers remarked that here Bismarck was on the wrong track, and would be compelled to retreat, with all his power. Bismarck was too wise a man to persist in attempting impossibilities, and after a bitter fight he became conciliatory. He did not "go to Canossa," but he yielded to the dictates of patriotism and enlightened policy, and the quarrel was patched up.

His long struggles with the Catholics told upon his health and spirits, and he was obliged to seek long periods of rest and recreation on his estates, — sometimes, under great embarrassments and irritations, threatening to resign, to which his imperial master, grateful and dependent, would never under any circumstances consent. But the prince president of the ministers and chancellor of the empire was loaded down with duties — in his cabinet, in his office, and in the parliament — most onerous to bear, and which no other man in Germany was equal to. His burdens at times were intolerable; his labors were prodigious, and the opposition he met with was extremely irritating to a man accustomed to have his own way in everything.

Another thing gave him great solicitude, taxed to the utmost his fertile brain; and that was the rising and wide-spreading doctrines of Socialism, — which was to Germany what Nihilism is to Russia and Fenianism was to Ireland; based on discontent, unbelief, and desperate schemes of unpractical reform, leading to the assassination even of emperors themselves. How to deal with this terrible foe to all governments, all laws, and all institutions was a most perplexing question. At first he was inclined to the most rigorous measures, to a war of utter extermination; but how could he deal with enemies he could neither see nor find, omnipresent and invisible, and unscrupulous as satanic furies, — fanatics whom no reasoning could touch and no laws control, whether human or divine? As experience and thought enlarged his mental vision, he came to the conclusion that the real source and spring of that secret and organized hostility which he deplored, but was unable to reach and to punish, were evils in government and evils in the structure of society, — aggravating inequality, grinding poverty, ignorance, and the hard struggle for life. Accordingly, he devoted his energies to improve the general condition of the people, and make the struggle for life easier. In his desire to equalize burdens he resorted to indirect rather than direct taxation, — to high tariffs and protective duties to develop German industry; throwing to the winds his earlier beliefs in the theories of the Manchester school of political economy, and all speculative ideas as to the blessings of free-trade for the universe in general. He bought for the government the various Prussian railroads, in order to have uniformity of rates and remove vexatious discriminations, which only a central power could effect. In short, he aimed to develop the material resources of the country, both to insure financial prosperity and to remove those burdens which press heavily on the poor.

On one point, however, his policy was inexorable; and that was to suffer no reduction of the army, but rather to increase it to the utmost extent that the nation could bear, — not with the view of future conquests or military aggrandizement, as some thought, but as an imperative necessity to guard the empire from all hostile attacks, whether from France or Russia, or both combined. A country surrounded with enemies as Germany is, in the centre of Europe, without the natural defences of the sea which England enjoys, or great chains of mountains on her borders difficult to penetrate and easy to defend, as is the case with Switzerland, must have a superior military force to defend her in case of future contingencies which no human wisdom can foresee. Nor is it such a dreadful burden to support a peace establishment of four hundred and fifty thousand men as some think, — one soldier for every one hundred inhabitants, trained and disciplined to be intelligent and industrious when his short term of three years of active service shall have expired: much easier to bear, I fancy, than the burden of supporting five paupers or more to every hundred inhabitants, as in England and Scotland.

In 1888 Bismarck made a famous speech in the Reichstag to show the necessity of Prussia's being armed. He had no immediate fears of Russia, he said; he professed to believe that she would keep peace with Germany. But he spoke of numerous distinct crises within forty years, when Prussia was on the verge of being drawn into a general European war, which diplomacy fortunately averted, and such as now must be warded off by being too strong for attack. He mentioned the Crimean war in 1853, the Italian war in 1858, the Polish rebellion in 1863, the Schleswig-Holstein embroilment which so nearly set all Europe by the ears, the Austro-Prussian war of 1866, the Luxemburg dispute in 1867, the Franco-German war of 1870, the Balkan war of 1877, the various aspects of the Eastern Question, changes of government in France, etc., — each of which in its time threatened the great "coalition war," which Germany had thus far been kept out of, but which Bismarck wished to provide against for the future.

"The long and the short of it is," said he, "that we must be as strong as we possibly can be in these days. We have the capability of being stronger than any other nation of equal population in the world, and it would be a crime if we did not use this capability. We must make still greater exertions than other Powers for the same ends, on account of our geographical position. We lie in the midst of Europe.

We have at least three sides open to attack. God has placed on one side of us the French, — a most warlike and restless nation, — and he has allowed the fighting tendencies of Russia to become great; so we are forced into measures which perhaps we would not otherwise make. And the very strength for which we strive shows that we are inclined to peace; for with such a powerful machine as we wish to make the German army, no one would undertake to attack us. We Germans fear God, but nothing else in the world; and it is the fear of God which causes us to love and cherish peace."

Such was the avowed policy of Bismarck, — and I believe in his sincerity, — to maintain friendly relations with other nations, and to maintain peace for the interests of humanity as well as for Germany, which can be secured only by preparing for war, and with such an array of forces as to secure victory. It was not with foreign Powers that he had the greatest difficulty, but to manage the turbulent elements of internal hostilities and jealousies, and oppose the anarchic forces of doctrinaires, visionary dreamers, clerical aggressors, and socialistic incendiaries, — foes alike of a stable government and of ultimate progress.

In the management of the internal affairs of the empire he cannot be said to have been as successful as was Cavour in Italy  He was not in harmony with the spirit of the age, nor was he wise. His persistent opposition to the freedom of the Press was as great an error as his persecution of the Catholics; and his insatiable love of power, grasping all the great offices of State, was a serious offence in the eyes of a jealous master, the present emperor, whom he did not take sufficient pains to conciliate.  The greatness of Bismarck was not as administrator of an empire, but rather as the creator of an empire, and which he raised to greatness by diplomatic skill.  His distinguishable excellence was in the management of foreign affairs; and in this power he has never been surpassed by any foreign minister.

Contrary to all calculations, this great proud man who has ruled Germany with so firm a hand for thirty years, and whose services have been unparalleled in the history of statesmen, was not too high to fall. He has fallen because a young, inexperienced, and ambitious sovereign, — apt pupil of his own in the divine right of monarchs to govern, and yet seemingly inspired by a keen sensitiveness to his people's wants and the spirit of the age, — could not endure his commanding ascendency and haughty dictation, and accepted his resignation offered in a moment of pique. He has fallen as Wolsey fell before Henry VIII., — too great a man for a subject, yet always loyal to the principles of legitimacy and the will of his sovereign But he retired at the age of seventy-five, with princely estates, unexampled honors, and the admiration and gratitude of his countrymen; with the consciousness of having elevated them to the proudest position in continental Europe, in spite of the dangers which have threatened them from the east and the west and the south, to say nothing of those arising from internal dissensions and parliamentary discords   The aged Emperor William I. died in 1888, full of years and of honors.   His son the Emperor Frederick died within a few months of him, leaving behind a deep respect and a genuine sorrow.   The grandson, the present Emperor William II., has been called "a modern man, notwithstanding certain proclivities which still adhere to him, like pieces of the shell of an egg from which the bird has issued."   He is yet an unsolved problem, but may be regarded not without hope for a wise, strong, and useful reign.

As for Prince Bismarck, with all his faults,—and no man is perfect,—I love and honor this courageous giant, who has labored, under such vexatious opposition, to secure the unity of Germany and the glory of the Prussian monarchy; who has been conscientious in the discharge of his duties, as he has understood them, in the fear of God, whose sovereignty he has ever, like his imperial master, acknowledged,—a modern Cromwell in another cause, whose fame will increase with the advancing ages.   The truly immortal men are those

who have rendered practical services to their country
and to civilization in its broadest sense, rather than
those theoretical dreamers who with fine sounding words
have imposed upon their contemporaries.

---

## AUTHORITIES.

Professor Seely's Life of Stein, Hezekiel's Biography of Bismarck,
and the Life of Prince Bismarck by Charles Lowe, are the books to which
I am most indebted for the compilation of this chapter.   But one may
profitably read the various histories of the Franco-Prussian war, the Life
of Prince Hardenberg, the Life of Moltke, the Life of Scharnhorst, and
the Life of William von Humboldt.   An excellent abridgment of German
History, during this century, is furnished by Professor Müller.   The
Speech of Prince Bismarck in the German Reichstag, February, 1888,
I have found very instructive and interesting, — a sort of resumé of his
own political life.

# PRINCE BISMARCK.

## A CHARACTER SKETCH.—By BAYARD TAYLOR.

### WRITTEN IN 1877.

# PRINCE BISMARCK.

## A CHARACTER SKETCH.—By BAYARD TAYLOR.

THE distinction between a politician and a statesman is constantly forgotten, or at least practically
slurred over, in our civil history.  The former may be
described as a man who studies the movements of
parties as they are developed from day to day, and
from year to year ; who is quick to avail himself of
popular moods and thereby to secure temporary power;
and whose highest success lies in his barometrical
capacity of foreseeing coming changes and setting the
sails of his personal fortune in such wise as either
safely to weather a gale or to catch the first breath of
a favorable wind.  But the statesman is one who is
able to look, both backward and forward, beyond his
own time ; who discovers the permanent forces under-
lying the transient phenomena of party conflicts ; who
so builds that, although he may not complete the
work, those who succeed him will be forced to complete
it according to his design; and who is individually
great enough to use popularity an an aid, without
accepting the lack of it as a defeat.

In the economy of human government, it so happens that very frequently mere politicians are elevated to seats which should be occupied, of right, by statesmen ; while the latter, shut out from every field of executive power, and allowed no other place than the parliamentary forum, are too often mistaken for mere political theorists.   The history of our own country gives us many examples of this perversity of fate, this unhappy difference between the path indicated by genius and that prescribed by circumstances.   But in Europe, where the accident of rank in almost all cases determines the possible heights of political power, the union of genius and its field of action—of statesmanship and opportunity—is much rarer.   And rarest of all is that grasp of mind which never fails to consider passing events in their broadest relation to all history, and that serenity of intellect which is satisfied with their logical place therein, though the present generation be incompetent to perceive it.   Of the six prominent European statesmen of this century—Pitt, Stein, Metternich, Cavour, Gortschakoff, and Bismarck—the last-named possesses these rare faculties in the fullest degree.   More fortunate than most of the others, he has lived to see much of his work secured—so far as our intelligence may now perceive—beyond the possibility of its being undone.

When the younger Pitt, early in 1806, after the

battles of Ulm and Austerlitz, cried out in despair, "Roll up the map of Europe!" he could not have guessed that in less than ten years his heroic although unfortunate policy would be triumphant. He died a few months afterwards, broken in spirit, with no prophetic visions of Leipsic and Waterloo to lighten his hopeless forebodings. Stein saw Germany free, but his activity ceased long before she rose out of the blighting shadow of the Holy Alliance; Metternich perished after the overthrow of the system to which he had devoted his life; and Cavour passed away nearly ten years before Venice and Rome came to complete his United Italy. Gortschakoff still lives,\* a marvel of intellectual vigor at his age, and may well rejoice in the emancipation of the serfs, the liberalization of the Russian Government, and the elevation of his country to a new importance in the world; but it has not been given to him, as to Bismarck, to create a new political system, to restore a perished nationality, and to fill its veins with blood drawn directly from the hearts of the people.

If Bismarck's career is so remarkable in its results, it is even more remarkable in its character. We can comprehend it only by estimating at their full value two distinct, almost antagonistic, elements which are

---

\* He died in 1883.

combined in his nature. It requires some knowledge
of the different classes of society in Germany, and of
the total life of the people, to understand them clearly;
and I must limit myself to indicating them in a few
rapid outlines.

Bismarck is of an ancient noble family of Pomerania, belonging to that class which is probably the
most feudalistic in its inherited habits, and the
most despotically reactionary in its opinions, of
the various aristocratic circles of Germany. In him
the sense of will and the instinct of rule which brooks
no disobedience are intensified by a physical frame of
almost giant power and proportions. He is one of
those men who bear down all obstacles from impulse,
no less than from principle—who take a half-animal
delight in trampling out a path when others attempt
to beset or barricade it. Apart from his higher political purposes, he cannot help but enjoy conquering for
the sake of conquest alone. This is not a feature of
character which implies heartlessness or conscious
cruelty; in him it coexists with many fine social,
humane, and generous qualities.

The other element in Bismarck's nature, which lifts
him so far above the level of the class into which he
was born, is an almost phenomenal capacity to see
all life and all history apart from his inherited intellectual tendencies. Until recently, it was almost

impossible for any Prussian *Junker* to judge a political question of the present day without referring
it to some obsolete, mediæval standard of opinion ; but
there never was an English or an American statesman
more keenly alive to the true significance of modern
events, to the importance of political movements and
currents of thought, and to the necessity of selecting
strictly practical means, than the Chancellor of the
German Empire. He possesses a wonderful clearness
of vision, and therefore rarely works for an immediate
result. In the midst of the most violent excitements
his brain is cool, for he has studied their causes and
calculated their nature and duration. It is impossible
that he should not have gone through many intellectual struggles in his early years : the opposing qualities which combine to form his greatness could not
have been easily harmonized. Out of such struggles,
perhaps, has grown a tact—or let us rather call it a
power—which specially distinguishes him. He possesses an astonishing skill in the use of an inscrutable
reticence or an almost incredible frankness, just as he
chooses to apply the one or the other ; and some of
his most signal diplomatic triumphs have been won
in this manner. The secret thereof is, that while he
uses the antiquated conventionalisms of diplomacy
when it suits, he relishes every fair opportunity of
showing his contempt for them by speaking the

simple truth, knowing beforehand that it will not be believed.

Looking back over his history, it is now easy to see that Bismarck's great political plan might easily have failed, had he not possessed such a remarkable combination of candor and secretiveness. It was undoubtedly slowly developed in his mind during his residence of eight years in Frankfurt as the representative of Prussia in the old German Diet. He there learned the impracticability of such a union, the damage inflicted upon all Germany by the dominant influence of Austria, and the necessity of a radical political change. His strong conservative sentiments did not blind him to the fact that such a change could only be accomplished by the aid of the people ; and this involved the danger, at that time, of precipitating a new revolution. He had the power to wait, and, while keeping his great object steadily in view, to conceal every movement which pointed towards it. Even had he been far more liberal in his political views, he could not have escaped the necessity of endeavoring to place himself at the head of the Conservative party: there was no other path to power, and no success was possible without power.

In other respects, his residence at Frankfurt was rich in opportunities for the broader education of a statesman. His journeys to Italy, Hungary, Den-

mark, and Holland, his wide acquaintance with intelligent representatives of all European nations, and
his acquisition of many languages, were aids to his
cool, objective study of races, events, and governing
forces.    There was little opportunity for personal
distinction; the character of his services was only
known to Frederic William IV. and his ministers;
but the former, if unsuccessful as a ruler, was a man
of great wit and keen intellect, and appreciated Bismarck's ability from the first.    Not until he was
appointed ambassador to Russia, in 1859, was the
future statesman much heard of, outside of Prussia.
His position in St. Petersburg, and afterwards in
Paris, made manifest his intellectual power and diplomatic skill, and brought his name into prominence.
When he became the minister of King William I.,
in the autumn of 1862, the moral shock which the
German people experienced was not caused by their
ignorance of his abilities.    He was by that time well
known, distrusted, feared, and—hated.

I can distinctly recall the excitements of this
period.    When I reached St. Petersburg, in June,
1862, Bismarck had taken his leave but a few weeks
previously, and the diplomatic and court circles still
included him in their gossip.    He was almost in-
variably spoken of with the greatest cordiality: his
frankness, good-nature, and hearty enjoyment of

repartee were specially emphasized. I remember that his brief term of service in France was then watched with very keen interest by the representatives of the other Powers. When I returned to Germany, a year later, he was at the head of affairs in Berlin ; and I doubt whether even Metternich was ever so unpopular with the great majority of the people. This was not surprising; for a member of the Prussian *Herrenhaus* (House of Lords), who was a chance travelling-companion of mine, expressed his unbounded satisfaction that an "Absolutist" was at last minister. There would be no more revolutions, he affirmed ; no more concession of useless privileges to the people ; the ancient rights of king and nobles would be restored. When the Conservatives said these things, the Liberals were justified in foreboding the worst evils. During this period I saw Bismarck, for the only time; and, however much I sympathized with the general feeling, I could not withhold the respect and admiration which attend the recognition of grand individual power. In stature and proportions he seemed to me to be the equal of General Winfield Scott, but his face had nothing of the vanity and petulance which characterized the latter's. It was massive, clear, and firm—as if cut in granite when in repose, but slowly brightening when he spoke. His tremendous will was expressed as fully in the large, clear gray eyes as in the outlines of the jaw. To judge from photographs, his face has changed but slightly since then.

The world will never know the extent of the strain to which Bismarck's nature was subjected during those four years, when he rarely looked upon the people without meeting gloomy eyes or hearing sullen murmurs of hate, when murder constantly tracked his footsteps and revolution only waited for some act which might let it loose. His long conflict with the Legislative Assembly, in regard to the army estimates, was inevitably misinterpreted. In fact, it was so designed ; for the statesman's secret plan could not be concealed from Austria, France, and Europe, unless the German people were first deceived. But the suspicion that the increase of the military power of Prussia was solely intended to create a weapon against the liberties of the people provoked an imminent danger. Bismarck walked on a narrow path between two abysses : if he had wavered for an instant, he must have fallen. He was made to feel, in a thousand ways, the depth of the popular indignation ; and he bore it, perhaps, the more easily because he always frankly declared his consciousness of it. This is a part of his experience which Herr Hesekiel * has passed over very lightly, out of consideration for the Germans them-

---

* In his authorized Biography of Bismarck.

selves, no less than for his subject; yet it should by no means be omitted from the statesman's biography. One incident, which I heard of at the time it occurred, is worth preserving. Bismarck was dining with a friend at the *table d'hôte* of a hotel in Frankfurt, when he noticed strong signs of hostile recognition in two ladies who sat opposite. They immediately dropped their German, and began talking in the almost extinct *Lettisch* (Lettonian) tongue, feeling themselves perfectly safe to abuse the minister to their heart's content therein. But Bismarck, who never forgets anything, remembered a few words of the language, and could guess the drift of their talk. He waited a while, and then whispered to his friend, " When I say something to you in an unknown tongue, hand me the dish of potatoes." Presently he spoke aloud, in Lettonian, "Give me the potatoes, please !" The friend instantly complied; the ladies stared, petrified with surprise, then hurriedly rose and left the table.

It is impossible wholly to preserve a great political secret from the instincts of other minds. For a year before the declaration of war against Austria, in 1866, a presentiment of something not entirely evil, to be reached through Bismarck's government, began to be felt in Germany. Singularly enough, it first impressed itself upon the young, and, when betrayed, was a frequent source of trouble in the homes of the Liberal party. Among other instances, a boy of my own acquaintance, not more than eighteen years of age, prevailed upon his fellow-pupils in an academy to join him in sending a letter of congratulation to Bismarck, after young Blind's mad attempt at assassination. He was rewarded by a charming letter from the minister, and in the pride of his heart could not help showing it, to the amazement and deep mortification of his parents. But now the noble young fellow is dead; and Bismarck's letter, preserved in a stately frame, is treasured by the family as a most precious souvenir of the son's foresight. The declaration of war nevertheless was a great shock to Germany. Even then its true purpose was not manifest; but six weeks of victory, and the conditions of peace, opened the eyes of all. It is difficult to find, in the annals of any nation, such an overwhelming revulsion of sentiment. The swiftness of the work gave convincing evidence of long preparation : it was a phenomenon in German politics ; and the truth pierced, like a sudden shaft of lightning, to the hearts and brains of the whole people. In a day, Bismarck the Despot was translated into Bismarck the Liberator.

When in Germany, in 1867, I learned, through the best sources, of a suggested *finale* to the Prusso-Austrian war, which I do not think has yet passed into history. The proposition, privately considered at

Nikolsburg before signing the treaty of peace with Austria, was that the entire Prussian army should march westward through Bavaria, Würtemberg, and Baden, to the Rhine, compel the support of Southern Germany, and engage France if she should take up the gage of battle thus thrown down. The boldness of such a plan must have made it very attractive ; but Bismarck, probably in deference to the King's views, finally declared that the fortune already secured was so great that it must not be hazarded. How much he gained by waiting four years does not now need to be explained. The movement might have been carried into effect, with very great probability of success; yet it would only have united Germany in form, not in feeling. It might have reconstructed the Empire, but upon no such firm foundation as it stands on at present.

From that day, all men in all civilized countries who study the development of history have followed with keenest interest the course of the German states- man. He has been the focus of such intelligent observation that no important line of policy could long be kept secret ; but it is still the habit to dis- trust his simplest and frankest declarations. A mind of lower order would have been satisfied with the enormous triumph of avenging those bitter years of the Napoleonic usurpation, from 1806 to 1813, with restoring the ancient boundaries of race after two centuries, and constructing the new and vital, because logical and coherent, German nationality.

It was known that Bismarck's iron constitution had been seriously shattered by his long and unrelieved labors and the tremendous wear and tear of his moral energy. He should now be satisfied, said the world; he has a right to a season of rest and peace. Therefore, when he immediately plunged into a new and—as many of his heartiest admirers believed—an unnecessary struggle, there was a general feeling of surprise, amounting almost to dissatisfaction. The simple truth is, he saw the beginning of a conflict which will continue to disturb the world until it is finally settled by the complete divorcement of Church and State in all civilized nations. The work he undertook to do had far less reference to the interests of our day than to those of the coming generations. I shall not discuss the means he employed : to do this intelligently requires an intimate knowledge of the history of the whole subject in Germany since the Treaty of Westphalia, in 1648 ; and hence very little of the foreign criticism of his policy is really applicable. He has at least succeeded in building a firm dike against the rising tide of ecclesiastical aggression; and the fight yet to be fought in France and Italy and Spain—perhaps even in England and the United

States—will be the less fierce and dangerous because
of his present work. He might well have avoided
the hard, implacable features of the struggle, but the
principle which impels him has the imperious character of a conscience.

While wondering at this man's great work, we
must nevertheless guard ourselves against attributing
to him liberal ideas of government in any partisan
sense. He is an aristocrat, lifted by a great intellect
above the narrowing influences of his rank. He
believes in a government of power, and which shall
exercise its power sternly when need comes. His
habit of facing events defiantly, even in cases where
a conciliatory policy might lead to the same results,
makes his attitude sometimes unnecessarily harsh and
despotic. As an individual, he is magnanimous ; as
a statesman, never. His exaction of terms from
France, his treatment of the German press, the
bishops, and finally Count von Arnim, are prominent
illustrations of this quality of his nature. In debate
he is sometimes carried too far by the irritation
created by his antagonists, and quite forgets his
acquired imperturbability. But even in such instances he often has courage enough to publicly confess the fault. The truth is, he accepts the legislative feature of the Imperial Government of Germany
through his intellect, while the inherited instincts of

his nature rebel against it. His brain is modern, but the blood which feeds it is that of the Middle Ages.

For compactness, clearness, and force there are no better speeches in the German language than Bismarck's. He is an excellent English scholar, and has evidently modelled his style upon the best English examples. His sentences are short and as little involved as possible : he endeavors to avoid that construction, peculiar to the German tongue, which throws the verb—often the key-word to the meaning —to the very end of the sentence. He is rarely eloquent; but he has an epigrammatic power of putting a great deal of significance into brief phrases, many of which find immediate currency among the people. For instance, the whole meaning of his conflict with the Catholic ecclesiastics was compressed into the sentence, "We shall not go to Canossa !" And the declaration of his policy of "blood and iron," which sent a thrill of horror through the country when first uttered, has become a proud and popular phrase..

Bismarck stands now [1887] at the height of his success. He can receive no additional honor, nor is it likely that his influence will be further extended, except through new developments which may attest the wisdom of his policy. It is not in his nature to stand idle : while he lives he will remain in action. He will therefore be a disturbing influence in European politics—an element of power through respect, or mistrust, or fear. But while it is not likely that any force or combination of forces can overthrow the work of his life, nothing he may henceforth do can invalidate his right to the title of the First Statesman of the Age.

NEW YORK, *March* 17, 1887.

# SPEECH OF BISMARCK

## BEFORE THE GERMAN REICHSTAG.

### FEBRUARY 6, 1888.

#### Translated by SARAH ZIMMERMAN.

IF I make use of words to-day, it is not to commend to your acceptance the measure * which the President has just mentioned. That it will be passed, I do not doubt; nor do I believe I can do anything to increase the majority by which it will be passed, and to which of course great importance is attached, both at home and abroad. Gentlemen of all parties will have settled their intentions as they are inclined, and I have the fullest confidence that the German Reichstag will again restore this increase of our defensive power to the height from which we gradually reduced it in the years 1867–1882; and this, not on account of the situation in which we now find ourselves, not on account of the apprehensions which the Stock Exchange and public opinion are able to excite, but as the result of a wise examination of the whole situation of Europe. Therefore I shall have more to say in my speech about this, than about the measure itself.

I do not care about speaking, for in this matter a word unfortunately spoken may do much harm, and many words

---

* Relating to an additional tax for the purpose of increasing the Imperial army.

cannot do much towards enlightening the minds of our
own people and the minds of foreigners. This indeed they
might themselves do without my aid. I speak unwillingly;
but I fear that were I to keep silent the expectations which
are attached to the present debate, the unrest in public
opinion, the anxious disposition of our people and of foreign
nations, would rather increase than decrease. It would be
thought that the question is so difficult and so critical that
a foreign minister dared not touch the situation. I speak,
therefore ; but I speak with reluctance.

I might confine myself to recalling expressions which I
made from this same place more than a year ago. The situation has changed but little since then. I came across a
newspaper cutting to-day from the *Freisinnige Zeitung*
["Freethinking Newspaper"]—a publication which, I believe, belongs more to my political friend Deputy Richter
[the Socialist] than to me [laughter]—which pictured a
tolerably knotty subject in order thereby to explain something more difficult. But I will only make general reference
to the main points cited there, with the declaration that if
the situation be altered since then, it is for the better rather
than for the worse.

A year ago we were afraid chiefly of a declaration of war
which might come to us from France. Since then a peace-
loving President has retired from the government in France,
and a peace-loving President has succeeded him. It is a
favorable symptom, that in its election of a new head of the
State the French Government has not put its hands into
Pandora's box, but that we may reckon that the peaceable
policy represented by President Grévy will be continued by
President Carnot. Besides this, we have other changes in the

French Ministry whose indication for peace is even stronger than the change of President, which was connected with other reasons. Such members of the ministry as were disposed to subordinate the peace of their country and of Europe to their personal plans have been pushed out, and others of whom we have not this fear have taken their places. I think I am also able to state—and I do it with much pleasure, because I wish not to rouse public opinion, but to quiet it—that our own attitude towards France appears more peaceful, much less explosive, than it has been for some years.

The fears which have arisen during this year have been directed much more towards Russia than towards France, or, I may say, towards the exchange of mutual agitations, threats, quarrels, and provocations, which have taken place between the Russian and French press in the course of the summer. But I do not believe that the question is altered in Russia from what it was a year ago. The "Freethinker" has printed prominently, with particularly black type, what I said last year:

"Our friendship with Russia suffered no break during the time of our war, and is raised above all doubt to-day. At all events, we expect from Russia neither an attack nor an unfriendly policy."

That this was printed in large type was perhaps intended to make the attack on it easier [laughter] ; perhaps also with the hope that I have arrived at a different opinion in the mean time, and am persuaded to-day that my trust in the Russian policy of last year was a mistake. That is not the case. That which makes it look so lies partly with the Russian press, partly in the mobilization of Russian troops.

Concerning the press, I cannot attach decided importance

to it.   They say that in Russia it is of more signification than
in France.   My opinion is exactly the contrary.   In France
the press is a power which exerts influence upon the resolu-
tions of the government; it is not so in Russia, nor can it
be : in both cases the press is for me but printer's ink upon
paper, against which we wage no war.   There lies no provoca-
tion for us in it.   Only one man stands behind every article
in the press,—he who has guided the pen that sends each
article into the world.   Even in a Russian paper—we assume
it to be an independent Russian paper—that is supported with
French secret funds, it is all the same.   The pen which writes
therein an article unfriendly to Germany is supported by
no one but him who has guided it with his hand—by no one
but him who has achieved this lucubration in his study, and
by the censor, which a Russian newspaper is bound to have ;
i.e., one of the more or less high officials in current politics,
who gives his protection only to this same Russian paper.
Both writer and censor have as little influence contrary to
the authority of His Majesty the Czar of Russia as the
weight of a feather.

In Russia the press has not the same influence upon public
opinion as in France, and at the most is its barometer, tol-
erated according to the standard of Russian press laws, but
without in any way attracting the attention of the Russian
Government, or of His Majesty the Czar of Russia.   As
against the opinion of the Russian press, I had the immediate
testimony of the Emperor Alexander himself.   When, after
the lapse of several years, I had the honor of being again received in audience by the Czar a few months ago, I again
convinced myself that the Emperor of Russia entertains no
warlike tendency toward us, has no intention either to invade

us, or to wage any aggressive war. I do not believe the Russian press; but I do believe the word of the Emperor Alexander, and absolutely trust it. If both lie on the scales before me, the testimony of the Russian press, with its hatred towards Germany, flies up in the air like a feather, while the personal testimony of the Emperor Alexander has great weight for me. Therefore I say, the press does not cause me to think that our relations with Russia to-day are worse than they were a year ago.

I come to the other question—that of the mobilization of Russian troops. Such movements have always taken place to a large extent; they have taken the present imaginary threatening form especially since 1879—since the end of the Turkish war. There may be, indeed, very slightly, an appearance that the accumulation of Russian troops in the neighborhood of the German and Austrian boundaries, in districts where their maintenance is dearer and more difficult than in the interior of their own country, can only suggest the intention of invading and seizing suddenly one of the neighboring countries, *sans dire: Gare!* *—I cannot find just the right German expression. But I do not think that to be the fact. For one thing, it is not characteristic of the Russian monarch; it is in contradiction to his utterances, and its object would be extraordinarily difficult to understand. Russia can have no intention of conquering part of Prussia; nor of Austria either, I believe. I think that Russia possesses quite as many Polish subjects as it wishes for, and it has no inclination to increase their numbers. [Laughter.]

No reason, no pretext, can be shown why any European

---

* "Without saying: On guard!"—an expression of the fencing-school.

sovereign should attack his neighbors quite suddenly. I go so far in my belief as to be persuaded that if, through any explosive phenomenon in France, upon which no one can reckon beforehand, and which the present government in France certainly does not expect—if we found ourselves entangled in a French war through such a phenomenon, Russia would not immediately join it. And, on the other hand, were we involved in a war with Russia, we should be quite safe from France ; no French Government would be strong enough to hinder it, however great its wish to do so. But again, to-day, I say that I look for no aggression from Russia, and retract nothing which I declared a year ago.

You will ask : Why, then, the mobilization of troops in this expensive manner ? Well, there are questions of which an explanation cannot easily be demanded from the foreign cabinets which they concern. When explanations are begun to be asked about them, ambiguous replies are given, and the rejoinder is again ambiguous. It is a dangerous road, which I do not care to tread. The mobilization of troops is, according to my judgment, an occurrence for which one nation cannot demand a categorical explanation,—or, using a student's expression, " cannot take to task for,"—but against which preparations can be made with reserve and foresight.

Therefore I can give no authentic reason for the motives of these Russian mobilizations. But I, who have been trusted with foreign and also with Russian diplomacy for a generation—I, as well as any one else, may make my own reflections about them ; and they take me so far as to make me assume that the Russian Cabinet has the conviction—and it will be well founded—that, in the next European crisis which may happen, the weight of the Russian voice in the diplomatic

Areopagus of Europe will carry so much more influence the stronger Russia is on the European boundary,—the farther to the west the Russian troops are situated. Russia would be ready just so much more quickly, either as ally or as adversary, if she keeps her principal troops, or at least a strong army, near her western boundaries.

For a long time this policy has guided the Russian reviews of troops. You will remember that even during the Crimean war a large army was waiting all the time in the Polish kingdom, which, had it been despatched to the Crimea at the right moment, would perhaps have given another turn to the war. On looking farther back in the past, it will be found that in the movement of 1830 Russia was unprepared and unfit for attack, because it had no troops in large numbers in the west of its empire. It is therefore unnecessary to draw the conclusion that there is an aggressive intention toward us because troops are massed in the western provinces (*sapadin Guberni*, as the Russians say). I suppose that a fresh Eastern crisis is expected at some time or other ; in order then to be ready to assert the Russian wishes with great weight, one does not need a standing army in Kazan, but farther westward.

But if an Eastern crisis do happen ? Yes; we have no surety about that. In my opinion we have had four crises in this century, deducting the lesser ones, and those which did not fully develop themselves : one in the year 1809, which ended with the treaty by which Russia ceded the Pruth boundary ; then in 1828 ;* in 1854, the Crimean war ; and in 1877 †—in periods of about twenty odd years apart. Why

---

* The war between Russia and Turkey, consequent upon the Greek Revolution.

† The Russo-Turkish Balkan war.

should the next crisis occur so much sooner, rather than after the same space of time, about 1899, some twenty-two years later? I prefer at least to consider it possible that the crisis will be deferred, and not made to happen immediately.

Besides, there are also other European events, which are bound to occur in the similar periods. For example, Polish insurrections. In former times we looked for one every eighteen to twenty years. Perhaps the desire to prevent them is one reason why Russia wishes to be so strong in Poland. Likewise, changes of government in France—they also occur every eighteen or twenty years ; and no one can deny that a change in the French Government may lead to a crisis which every interested power must wish to be able to interfere in, with full importance—I mean only in a *diplomatic* manner, but with a diplomacy behind which stands an army perfectly equipped and ready to fight.

If Russia means this,—which I would much sooner conjecture from the standpoint of a purely technical, diplomatic judgment, based upon my experience, than that it wishes to respond to the comparatively hounding threats and bullyings of the newspapers,—there is absolutely no reason why we should look gloomily into our future, as we have generally done for the last forty years. The Eastern crisis is the most probable one that can happen. When it happens, we are not the most interested parties in it. Without approaching too nearly into any engagement, we are completely ready to wait while the powers most interested in the Mediterranean, in the Levant, first fight out their determinations, and then, as they prefer, strike or make peace with Russia.

We are not interested, in the highest degree, on one side or the other of the Eastern question. Every Great Power which seeks to interfere and to influence and to manage matters beyond its sphere of interest in the politics of other lands, ventures beyond the province which God has assigned to it; it follows the policy of power, and not the policy of interest; it governs for prestige only. We will not do that; we will wait, when the Eastern crisis comes, to see what situation the more interested Powers will take, before we make any movement.

There is therefore no reason to consider our situation at this moment so serious that just the present condition of affairs is the occasion on account of which we seek to-day to pass a military measure for a powerful increase of the army. I wish to keep aside the question of the second conscription of the militia; in short, to separate the measure for the increase of the army with the other, the financial bill, entirely from the question of what our present situation is. The question is not one of a merely temporary contrivance: it is one of a lasting, of a permanent, strengthening of the German army.

That it is not a question of a temporary arrangement, will be apparent, I believe, when I beg you to go with me through the alarms of war which we have had during the last forty years, without having been proved at any time to have been in a state of nervous restlessness. In the year 1848, when the dikes and sluices, which had till then confined the waters in their quiet courses, fell to pieces, we had to settle two matters which threatened war: they concerned Poland and Schleswig-Holstein. The first cry after the month of March was: War against Russia for the restoration of Poland! Soon after there was exceeding danger of becoming entangled in a great European war, through the

Schleswig-Holstein question ; and I do not need to recall to you how, through the settlement at Olmütz in 1850, a great conflagration was prevented.    There followed perhaps two years of a quieter time, but they were full of uneasiness.    It was at the time that I was minister in Frankfurt.

In the year 1853 the beginnings of the Crimean war were felt ; this war lasted from 1853 till 1856.    During the whole time we found ourselves on the very edge—I will not say of the precipice, but of the slope, down which we might be drawn into the war.    I remember that from 1853 till 1856 I was obliged to go backward and forward, like a pendulum, between Frankfurt and Berlin, because His late Majesty, by the confidence which he placed in me, really used me as deputy for his independent policy when the Western Powers were too strong in their persuasions that we, on our part, should also declare war against Russia, and the opposition of his minister of foreign affairs was too weak for him.    I do not know how often it was—the game tired me out—that I had to write a more friendly despatch to Russia for His Majesty ; that this despatch was sent off ; that Herr von Manteuffel sent in his resignation ; and that, after the despatch was gone, His Majesty begged me to go on an errand to Herr von Manteuffel, in the country or anywhere, and induce him to take up his portfolio again.    All the time was the Prussia of that day on the eve of a great war : it was exposed to the enmity of all Europe except Russia if it declined to agree with the policy of the Western Powers, and otherwise it would have been forced to a breach with Russia, —lasting probably for a long time, because the desertion of Prussia would have been felt most painfully by Russia.    During the Crimean war, then, we were in constant danger of being drawn in. That lasted till 1856, when it was finally concluded by the Treaty of Paris, and made for us, by this treaty, a kind of Canossa in the Paris Congress. There was no necessity for us to play the part of a greater Power than we were, and to ratify that treaty. But we bowed and scraped in order to be allowed finally to sign. That will not happen to us again. [Laughter.]

That was in 1856. As early as 1857 the Neuchâtel question threatened us with war, although it has not become very well known. At that time I was sent to Paris, in the spring of 1857, by the late King, in order to negotiate with the Emperor Napoleon about the marching through of Prussian troops to an attack upon Switzerland. What that meant, had it been agreed to, how it would have become a far-spreading war panic, how it would have led us into difficulties with France as well as with other Great Powers, every one will see to whom I tell it. The Emperor Napoleon did not feel inclined to consent to it. My negotiations in Paris were cut short, because His Majesty the King had in the mean time himself arranged the matter in a friendly way between Austria and Switzerland.*

But in that same year there was still danger of war. I may say that when I was in Paris on that mission the Italian war, which broke out somewhat more than a year later, was already in the air, and that we escaped almost by a hair's-breadth from being drawn into a great European coalition war. We went as far as starting troops: indeed, we should undoubtedly have attacked had not the Peace of

* Neuchâtel was detached from Prussia and became a member of the Swiss Confederation.

Villafranca been concluded—not at all too soon for Austria,
perhaps just at the right moment for us.  We should have
had to conduct war under unfavorable conditions ; we should
have had to turn a campaign which was Italian into a
Prusso-French war, the conclusion, end, and treaty of which
would not have depended upon us, but upon the friends or
enemies who stood behind us.  And so, with the war-clouds
leaving the horizon clear for one year, we reached the
Sixties.

In 1863 occurred a scarcely less great danger of war, which
remains comparatively unknown to the great public, and
which will first make an impression when the secret archives
of the Cabinet are published.  You will remember the Polish
rebellion, which happened in 1863 ; and I shall never forget
how one morning, during one of the visits from Sir Andrew
Buchanan, the English ambassador, and Talleyrand, the
French representative, which I was wont to have, they made
hell hot for me about the inexcusable adhesion of the Prussian policy to that of Russia, and spoke rather menacingly to
us.  Later at noon of the same day I had the pleasure of
hearing in the Prussian Landtag the same arguments and
charges with which the two foreign ministers had attacked
me in the morning.  [Laughter.]  I could have stood that
quietly ; but the Emperor Alexander lost patience, and wished
to draw the sword against the chicanery of the Western
powers.  You will remember that the French forces were
then engaged in Mexico with American projects, so that
France could not put forth its whole power.  The Tzar of
Russia would not any longer submit to the Polish intrigues
carried on by the other powers, and was prepared in alliance
with us to resist events and strike.  You will remember that

at that time Prussia internally was in a difficult position—
that in Germany minds were already fermenting, and Frankfurt's assembly of princes was in preparation. It must be
acknowledged that there existed a great temptation for my
gracious master to settle this difficult internal question by
entering upon a warlike undertaking in great style; and
doubtless there would have been war by Prussia and Russia
in alliance against those who supported the Polish rebellion
against us, had not His Majesty been held back by a dread of
solving internal difficulties, Prussian as well as German, with
outside help ["Bravo!"]; and we declined,—silently, without
asserting the reasons for our proceedings beyond the unfriendly projects of other German Governments toward us.
The death of the King of Denmark soon afterward turned all
interested persons to other thoughts. But it required only a
"Yes" instead of a "No" at Gastein from His Majesty, and
a great war, the coalition war, would have happened in 1863.
Any other but a German minister would probably, as oppor-
tunist, have been persuaded by all considerations of utili-
tarianism, in order to solve our internal difficulties. Among
our own people, as well as among foreigners, there was
scarcely a right idea of the extent to which the will of the
nation and a faithful conscientiousness ["Bravo!" from the
Right] guided monarch and minister in the government of
the German country. ["Bravo!" from all sides.]

The year 1864—we were just speaking of 1863—brought
fresh and most alarming fears of war. From the moment
our troops crossed the Eider I was waiting each week for the
interference of the European convention of seniors [laughter]
in the Danish affair, and you will admit that it was in the
highest degree possible. Even at that time we could perceive

that if Austria and Germany were united, although the then existing German Confederation did not by any means have the same military signification which the same countries have to-day, they could not have been so easily attacked by Europe. ["Bravo!"] That was manifest even then; but the fear of war remained the same.

In 1865 the front changed, and preparations for the war of 1866 were then begun. I remember only one council of Prussian ministers which took place in 1865, after the occupation of Gueldres, which was afterwards vacated through the Treaty of Gastein. But in the year 1866 war fully broke out, and there was the greatest danger—which we prevented only through the most prudent use of circumstances—that out of this duel between Prussia and Austria a vast European coalition war might arise, in which the very question of existence would depend on brain and brawn.

That was 1866, and in 1867 the Luxembourg question followed. A somewhat firmer answer was then required from us —which perhaps we could have given, had we then been strong enough to have foreseen a good result with safety in bringing about the great French war at that time.

From thence onward, in 1868, 1869, till 1870, we were continuously in fear of war, while abiding by treaties which Herr von Beust made at the time in Salzburg and other places between France, Italy, and Austria, and about which care was taken that they should be performed at our cost. Apprehension before the [French] war was so great, that I as Prime Minister received many deputations from trading and industrial bodies, who said to me: "This indecision is quite unbearable; go to war rather: rather war than longer worry with this depression in all trades." We waited quietly till we were attacked ; and I believe we did well so to contain ourselves that we remained the aggressed and not the aggressors.

Now, since that great war of 1870 was fought, I ask you, Has there been any year without the fear of war? At the beginning of the Seventies—even as we came home from France—it was asked : "When will the next war be? When will the Revanche be fought? At latest in five years?" It was said to us then : "The question whether we are to have this war, and with what result "—it was one of the Hundred, who upbraided me with it in the Reichstag,—" depends nowadays only on Russia ; Russia alone has the sword in the hand." I shall probably return to this question later on.

In the mean time I wish to go on through the forty years' picture, and mention that again in 1876 a war-storm gathered : in 1877 the Balkan war would have led to a conflagration through the whole of Europe, and was prevented only by the Congress held in Berlin ; and quite suddenly after the Congress a new danger was opened up to us in the East, because Russia had taken amiss our behavior at the Congress. Perhaps I will come back again to that also, if my strength will allow me.

Then there followed a certain reaction in the intimate relationship of the three Emperors, which for some time had permitted us to look into the future with more quietude ; yet on the first symptoms of uncertainty in the relations between the three Emperors, or from the expiration of the treaties which they had made with each other, public opinion became nervous again. However, the overwrought excitement with which we struggle to-day, and have struggled during late years, but especially to-day, I hold to be particularly baseless.

Yet though I consider this nervousness to-day to be with-

out reason, I am far from drawing the conclusion from that
fact that we do not need to strengthen our forces for fighting.
On the contrary.  It is for this that I have unrolled this forty
years' tableau,—perhaps not to your amusement,—and I beg
pardon for it ; but had I omitted a year from that which
you yourselves have all so direfully experienced, there would
have been no idea that the state of anxiety before great wars,
before further complications the different entanglements of
which no one can judge beforehand, had been so prevalent
among us.  But now we must be prepared for it, once for
all.  Independently of the present situation, we must be so
strong, that with the consciousness of a great nation, which
is strong enough under any circumstances to hold its fortune
in its own hand against every coalition [" Bravo !"]; with
the confidence in itself and in God, which brings its own
power ; with the righteousness of our cause, which the care-
fulness of the government will endeavor to keep on the side
of Germany—we shall be able to look forward to every possibility, and to look forward with peace.  [" Bravo !"]

The long and the short of it is, that we must be as strong as
we possibly can in these days, and we have the capability of
being stronger than any other nation of equal population in
the world ! [" Bravo !"]—I will come back again to that,—and
it would be a crime if we did not use that capability.  If we
do not want our soldiers, we do not need to call them out.
It only depends upon the not very important question of
money—not very important, though I mention it by the way.
I have no inclination to enter upon military or financial
figures, but during the last few years France has invested
three thousand millions in the improvement of her forces,
while we have hardly spent fifteen hundred millions, including

that which we now ask from you. ["Hear! hear!" from the Right.] However, I will leave this to the Ministers of War and of the Finance Department to put forward.

When I say we must be continually trying to be ready for all eventualities, I advance with that the claim that we must make still greater exertions than other powers for the same ends, on account of our geographical situation. We lie in the middle of Europe. We have at least three fronts open to attack. France has only her eastern boundary, Russia only her western side, on which they can be attacked. We are, besides, more exposed than any other people through our geographical situation to the danger of coalition and through the perhaps decreasing lack of cohesion, which the German nation has had up till now, in comparison with others. God has placed us in a situation in which we can be hindered by our neighbors from falling anyhow into slothfulness or dreaming. He has placed on one side of us the French—a most warlike and restless nation; and he has allowed the fighting tendencies of Russia, which did not exist to any extent in the earlier part of the century, to become great. So in a certain measure we get spurs from both sides, and are forced into a struggle which perhaps we would not otherwise make. The pikes in the European carp pond prevent us from becoming carp [laughter], because they let us feel their stings in both our sides. They force us to a struggle which probably we should not engage in of our own will; they also force us to a cohesion among us Germans which is opposed to our innermost nature [laughter]: otherwise we would rather struggle with each other. But the Franco-Russian press between which we have been taken compels us to hold together, and will materially increase our capability for cohesion through compression, till we reach the condition of indivisibility which is peculiar to almost all other nations, but which has failed us till now. [" Bravo ! "] And we must respond to this dispensation of Providence by making ourselves so strong that the pike can do no more to us than wake us up. [Laughter.]

Years ago we had the Holy Alliance. I remember an old American song which I learnt from my deceased friend Motley ; it begins :

" In good old colonial time,
    When we lived under a king."

Now those days of the Alliance were patriarchal times, when we had a number of provinces on which we could depend, and a number of dikes which protected us from the wild European floods. There was the German Confederation ; and the true beginning and continuation and consummation of the German Confederation, for whose use it was formed, was the Holy Alliance. We depended on Russia and Austria, and in all circumstances we were safe. We dwelt in a becoming shyness, on account of which we never ventured an opinion until the others had spoken. [Laughter.] That is all lost to us [" Very good !" from the Right] ; we must now help ourselves. The Holy Alliance suffered shipwreck in the Crimean war—not through our fault. The German Confederation was destroyed through us, because the existence which it created for us could not be borne long either by us or by the German people. Both have passed out of the world. After the dissolution of the German Confederacy, at the end of the war of 1866, Prussia, or the North Germany of that time, would have been isolated had we been forced to count

upon the fact that no one from any side would forgive us
the new issues, the important advances which we had obtained by great efforts.  Other powers never love to see the
success of their neighbors.

But our relations with Russia were not disturbed through
the affair of 1866.  In that year the remembrance of Count
Buol's policy, of Austria's policy during the Crimean war, was
still too fresh in Russia to allow the thought to arise there of
backing the Austrian monarchy against Prussian attack, of
renewing the campaign which the Emperor Nicholas had conducted in 1849 on behalf of Austria,—I beg to be excused if
I sit down for a moment ; I cannot stand any longer ;—therefore there is always for us a most natural affinity toward
Russia, which, anticipated in the last century, has taken an
acknowledged origin in the policy of the Emperor Alexander
I. in this century.  Indeed, Prussia owed him thanks.  In
1813 he could just as well have turned round on the Polish
frontiers and have concluded peace ; later on he could have
caused Prussia to fall.  In fact, for the restoration to the old
footing we really had to thank the good wishes of the Czar
Alexander I., or, if you will be sceptical, say the good wishes
of the Russian policy, for the way it used Prussia.

This gratitude has governed the reign of Frederick William
III.  The balance which was due to Russia on the Prussian
account has been used up in the friendship—I may almost
say in the service—which Prussia rendered during the whole
reign of the Czar Nicholas ; and I can say that it was settled
at Olmütz.*  At Olmütz the Czar Nicholas did not take the

* At the conference between Austria, Prussia, and Russia for
settling German discussions consequent upon the revolutionary
movement of 1848.

side of Prussia, did not once protect us from unfortunate experiences, from some humiliations ; for, taken on the whole, the Czar Nicholas had a stronger predilection for Austria than for Prussia ; the thought that we owed any thanks whatever to Russia during his reign is an historical legend.

But so long as the Czar Nicholas lived, we on our side did not break the tradition with Russia ; during the Crimean war, as I have already related to you, we held fast to the Russian side at considerable hazard and under threats. His Majesty the late King had no inclination to play—what then, as I believe, would have been possible—a decided rôle in the war with a strong army. We had concluded treaties by which we were bound at a certain time to bring forward 100,000 men on the field. I proposed to His Majesty to bring forward, not 100,000, but 200,000, and to mount them, so that we could use them right and left ; so that with His Majesty would have lain the final decision of the war. However, the late king was not inclined to warlike undertakings, and the people can only be grateful to him for it. I was younger and less experienced than I am to-day, However, we never bore rancor for Olmütz during the Crimean war : we came out of it as Russia's friend ; and during the time that I was ambassador in St. Petersburg I was able to enjoy the fruit of this friendship in a very welcome reception at court and in society. Our partisanship for Austria during the Italian war did not meet with the approval of the Russian Cabinet of that day, but it had no subsequent disadvantageous effect. Our war of 1866 [with Austria] was looked upon rather with a certain satisfaction ; Russia did not grudge Austria that, at that time. In 1870, during our French war, we had at least the satisfaction, coincidently with our defense and victorious advance, of being able to render a service to our Russian friend in the Black Sea. In no way could the Black Sea have been possibly opened by the contracting parties if the German troops had not stood victoriously in the neighborhood of Paris. For example, had the Germans been defeated, I believe the result of the London agreement would not have been given so easily in Russia's favor. From the war of 1870, therefore, no uneasiness remained between us and Russia.

I quote these facts in order to demonstrate to you the origin of the treaty [of 1879] with Austria, which was published only a few days ago, and to vindicate the policy of His Majesty from the reproach that it has enlarged the possibilities of war for the German Empire through that which concerns Austria and does not affect Germany. I intend, therefore, to describe to you how it has happened that the traditional relations between us and Russia, which I have always specially fostered, have taken such a form that we have been induced to publish the Austrian treaty made public the day before yesterday.

The earlier years after the French war were passed in the best understanding. In 1875 an inclination of my Russian colleague, Count Gortschakoff, came to light, of taking the trouble to win for himself more popularity with France than with us, and by using certain favorable contemporary coincidences to that end, in order to make the world believe by a telegram, prepared for the purpose,—as if in 1875 we had any such remote intention,—that we had intended to attack France, and it was through the wisdom of Prince Gortschakoff that France had been saved from this danger. That was the first estrangement that arose between us, and which led me to a lively exchange of sentiments with my former friend and later colleague.

At the same time we always held strongly to the question of firmly maintaining peace between the three emperors, of continuing the relations which first originated during the visits of the Emperors of Russia and of Austria in 1872 here in Berlin, and during the following return visits. We also succeeded in it.  In 1876, just before the Turkish war, we declined certain persuasions to an option between Russia and Austria, which were brought before us.  I do not consider it necessary to go through the details ; they were known at the time.  The effect of our refusal was, that Russia turned directly to Vienna, and a treaty—I believe it was in January, 1877—was concluded between Austria and Russia which affected the eventualities of an Eastern crisis, and for which, in such a case as the occupation of Bosnia, and so on, Austria provided.

Then came the [Russo-Turkish Balkan] war, and we were quite contented when the storm passed over even farther south than it was originally inclined to.  The end of the war was definitely settled here in Berlin by the Congress, after having been prepared by the Peace of San Stefano.  According to my conviction, the Peace of San Stefano was not much more hazardous for the anti-Russian powers, and not much more beneficial to Russia, than the later treaty of the Congress has been.  One may say the Peace of San Stefano reappeared subsequently of its own accord, because little East Roumelia, including some 800,000 souls altogether, I believe, arbitrarily took upon itself the restitution of the—*not quite* —of the old San Stefano limits, and annexed itself to Bulgaria.  Therefore the adjustment of the average, which the Congress established on the basis of San Stefano, was not so very bad. Whether or not the settlement of San Stefano were exactly a masterpiece of diplomacy, I leave undecided.

We had as little inclination to mix ourselves then in the Eastern question as we have to-day. I was dangerously ill in Friedrichsruhe, when the request was officially communicated to me on the part of Russia to convene a Congress of the Great Powers at Berlin for the definite settlement of the war. I had next to no inclination for it, partly because I was physically unable, but also because I had no desire to entangle ourselves so far in the matter as the rôle of President of a Congress necessarily involves. When, notwithstanding, I finally complied, it was partly owing to the German sense of duty toward the interests of peace, but specially owing to the grateful remembrance of the favor of the Czar Alexander II. toward me which I have always had, and which caused me to fulfill this wish. I declared myself ready, if we succeeded in obtaining the consent of England and of Austria. Russia undertook to get England's consent, I took upon myself to promise it for Vienna ; we succeeded, and the Congress was held.

During the Congress, I may truly say, I fulfilled my rôle so successfully, as far as I could in every way without hurting the interests of our own country or of our friends, that I might have been the fourth Russian plenipotentiary at this Congress [laughter] ; indeed, I may almost say, the third ; for I can scarcely acknowledge Prince Gortschakoff as a plenipotentiary of Russian policy, represented as it was by the real ambassador, Count Shouvaloff. [Laughter.]

During the whole of the business of the Congress no Rus-

sian wish came to my knowledge which I did not recommend ;
yea, which I did not carry through. In consequence of the
confidence which the lamented Lord Beaconsfield placed in
me, in the most difficult, most critical moment of the Congress, I appeared at his sick bed in the middle of the night,
and, at the moment when the Congress stood near a rupture,
obtained his signature in bed. In fact I so acted at the Congress, that when it was ended I thought, "I have long possessed the highest Russian Order in precious stones, otherwise
I should get it now." [Laughter.] In short, I had the feeling
that I had performed such a service for a foreign power as
is seldom permitted the minister of another country.

What, then, must have been my surprise and my amazement
as gradually a kind of press campaign commenced in St.
Petersburg, during which the German policy was attacked,
and I personally, through my intentions, was suspected !
These attacks increased during the following year, till in 1879
there were made strong claims that we should exercise upon
Austria a pressure in matters where we could not attack the
just rights of that country. I could not lend my hand to that ;
for had we estranged Austria from us, it would have happened, if we did not wish to be quite isolated in Europe, that
we should have been obliged to depend on Russia. Would
such a dependence have been endurable ? In former years I
should have believed it to be have been, for I should have
said to myself, "We have no mutual interests to quarrel
about ; there is no reason whatever why Russia should give
up our friendship." At least, I would not have directly
contradicted my Russian colleague, who had explained it all
to me. The occurrence concerning the Congress undeceived
me. It showed me that even a full surrender of our policy

(for a certain time) in favor of the Russian policy would not protect us from falling into war with Russia against our will and our endeavors.  This fight over instructions which we gave, or did not give, to our representatives at the negotiations in the south amounted to threats, to real threats of war, from the quarter least justified.

That is the origin of our treaty with Austria.  We were compelled through these threats to that option which I avoided ten years ago, of choosing between those two, who up till then had been our friends.  At that time, in Gastein and Vienna, I arranged the treaty which was published the day before yesterday, and which to-day still holds good between us.

Its publication, as I saw yesterday and the day before, is wrongly understood by the newspapers : they seek to find in it an ultimatum, a warning, a threat.  That signifies so much the less, as the text of the treaty has long been known to the Russian Cabinet.  Before November of last year we considered it due to the candor of a loyal monarch, such as the Czar of Russia is, as early as possible to leave him no doubt how matters lay.  I do not consider it possible *not* to have concluded this treaty ; if we had not arranged it then, we must have done so to-day.  It has exactly the chief attribute of an international treaty ; namely, it is the expression of the permanent interests of both sides—as much of the Austrian side as of ours. ["Bravo !"]  No Great Power is obliged to keep to the text of any treaty in opposition to the interests of its own people ; it is at last compelled to declare quite openly, "Times have altered ; I cannot hold to this any longer."  It must justify its course as well as possible with its own people, and with those who have concluded the treaty.  It is no credit to any Great Power to lead its own people into trouble because it keeps to the letter of one condition or another of a signed agreement. That will not be the case, anyway, with these treaties. They are just ;—not only the treaty which we have concluded with Austria, but similar treaties which exist between us and other governments ["Hear ! hear !" from the Right]—especially the treaties we have made with Italy : they are only the expression of mutual interest in the struggles and risks which nations have to run. Italy as well as ourselves has been in the situation of having to fight Austria for the right of consolidating itself nationally. Both live now at peace with Austria, and in common with Austria have the same struggles and dangers, which alike threaten peace, as precious to the one as to the other ; alike have to protect internal developments to which they would fain devote themselves, and to guard themselves from attacks. This endeavor, and with it the mutual confidence that the treaties will be kept, and that with these treaties neither party is bound to the other unless it is compatible with its own interests—all this makes these treaties firm, strong, and lasting. ["Bravo !"]

How much our treaty with Austria is the expression of the interests of both sides was shown at Nicolsburg, and in 1870. Even in the transactions at Nicolsburg we were under the impression that we could not do without Austria—and a strong, courageous Austria, which will endure in Europe. In 1870, when war broke out between us and France, the temptation was indeed extraordinarily strong for her susceptible feelings to use the opportunity, and take revenge on the enemy of 1866 ; but the thoughtful and prudent policy of the Austrian Cabinet was obliged to ask itself: "What would be the consequences ? In what situation should we find ourselves if we now ally ourselves to the French in order to conquer Prussia,—not to say Germany?" What would have been the consequences if France with Austria's help had conquered us ? Austria could have had by such a policy scarcely any other object than again taking its early position in Germany—for that was really the only reason it gave in 1866 ; there were no other reasons, those relating to pecuniary matters being quite unimportant. Now, what would the situation of Austria in the German Confederation as presidential power have been like, if it had been obliged to say that, in agreement with France, it had taken the left bank of the Rhine from Germany ; that it had again reduced the South German States to a Rhenish confederation dependent on France ; and that it had irrevocably condemned Prussia to look for Russia's support and to dependence on Russia's future policy ? Such a situation was unacceptable to the Austrian statesmen, who were not entirely blinded by rage and revenge.

But that is also the case with us in Germany. If you imagine Austria taken off the map of Europe, you will find that we, with Italy, are isolated between Russia and France—between the two strongest military powers next to Germany. We should either be one nation against two, or, very probably, changing our dependence from one to the other. It cannot be so. One cannot imagine Austria out of the way ; such an empire as Austria will not disappear. But such a nation as Austria will be estranged if left in the lurch, as was done at the Treaty of Villafranca, and will be inclined to offer its hand to those who, on their side, have been the antagonists of an unreliable friend.

In short, if we would guard against the isolation which, in the defenseless situation of Germany is particularly dangerous, we must have a sure friend.  We have, by virtue of similarity of interests, by virtue of this treaty which has been laid before you, two true friends—true, not out of love to each. other ;  for nations wage war on each other from hatred : it has never yet happened that out of love one country has sacrificed itself for another.  [Laughter.]  Hatred does not always lead to war.  If that were the case, France would be engaged in continuous wars, not only with us, but also with England and Italy ;  for it hates all its neighbors.  [Applause and consent.]   I do not believe that the dislike now expressed toward us in Russia is more than factitiously padded out, or will be of long duration.  Not only do opinions and friendships unite us with our allies of the treaty, but the most weighty interests of the European balance of power, and of our own future.

Therefore I think you will approve the policy of His Majesty the Emperor, which has led to the conclusion of this treaty [" Bravo ! "], even should the possibility of war be strengthened thereby.

It is quite true that the alliance we have made will be extraordinarily strengthened on one side by the passing of this bill, because the proposed increase in one department will exceedingly strengthen the German Empire itself.

The bill asks for an increase of armed troops,—a possible increase, which unless needed we shall not want to call out : it can remain at home.   But if we have it at our disposition, if we have arms for it,—(and that is thoroughly necessary : I remember the carbine supplied by England to our Landwehr in 1813, with which I practised as a sportsman—

that was no weapon for war. We cannot indeed procure weapons on the instant. But,) if we have arms for the purpose, this new law becomes a reinforcement for the security of peace, and a corroboration of the alliance for peace, which is as strong as if a fourth Great Power had joined the alliance with an army of 700,000 men—the highest number there ever was. ["Bravo!"]

I believe, also, that this large increase of strength will have a soothing effect upon our own people, and will abate in some measure the nervousness of public opinion, of the Bourse, and of the press. I hope they will feel comfort [laughter], if they make it clear to themselves that after this reinforcement, and from the moment it is signed and published, the soldiers are there. But there is a great want of arms; we must provide better ones, for if we would build up an army of "Triarians,"* of the best material that we have among our people, of men over thirty years of age, generally fathers of families, we must have the best kind of weapons for them that can be found anywhere. ["Bravo!"] We must not send them into battle with those which we do not consider good enough for our young recruits of the line. ["Very good!"] The capable men, the heads of households, these giants who still remind us of the time when they had possession of the bridge of Versailles, must certainly have the best weapon on their shoulders, the most complete arm, the most comfortable dress for protection against storms and all extreme events. [Repeated "Bravo!"] We dare not economize in this. And I hope it will quiet our fellow-countrymen if they now think

---

* Triarii : veteran Roman soldiers, who formed the third rank from the front when in order of battle.

it really likely to be the case (which I do not believe) that we should be attacked on both sides at one time.  As I explained to you in the history of the forty years, it is a possibility, for all imaginable coalitions may occur.  If it should happen, we could place a million good soldiers on the defensive on our borders.  At the same time we should be able to hold in reserve half a million or more, almost another million, in the background, and put them forward according to need.

It has been said to me, "This will only have the effect of causing the others to increase their armies."  But they cannot do that.  ["Bravo!"—Laughter.]  They have long reached their total amount.  We lowered the age in 1867, because we believed that, having the German Confederacy, we could make matters easier for ourselves, and could let men over thirty-two be free.  In consequence, our neighbors adopted a longer time for service, some a twenty-years period,—when the Minister of War speaks he will be able to explain it better to you ;—in number they are quite as many as we are, but they cannot approach us for quality.  ["Quite right!"]  Courage is the same in all civilized nations ; the Russian, the Frenchman, fights just as bravely as the German ; but our people—our 700,000 men—have served in war, are well-tried soldiers, who have not yet forgotten their profession.  And we have that in which no other people in the world can equal us—we have the material for officers and under-officers to command this immense army.  ["Bravo!"]  No other nation can approach us there.  To this end is directed the whole particular course of the education of the people in Germany ; and it is done in no other country.  The class of education which is necessary in order to fit an officer and a sub-officer to command, according to the claims which the soldier makes on him, is very much

higher here than in any other country. We have not only
more materials for officers and under-officers than any other
country, but we have a corps of actual officers which no other
nation in the world can equal. ["Bravo!"] In this, and also
in the excellence of our corps of non-commissioned officers,
who really are embryo officers, lies our superiority. The
course of education which an officer pursues not only makes
very urgent demands on his character, requiring self-denial
of luxuries and society, but makes the performance of social
tasks exceedingly difficult; the performance of which is
necessary, nevertheless, in order to encourage the fellowship
which—God be thanked—exists among us in the highest
degree, and which excites emulation between men and officers
without in any way injuring discipline.

No others can equal us in the relationship which exists in
the German army between officers and men, especially during
the time of war, with but few unfortunate exceptions—*Ex-
ceptio firmat regulam.* On the whole we can say : No German officer leaves his soldiers in the lurch under fire, but
fetches him out, even with danger to his own life ; and, *vice
versa*, no German soldier forsakes his officer : this we know
by experience. ["Bravo!"]

If other armies with the same number of troops that we
intend to have forthwith, will have officers and under-officers,
they will be compelled, under the circumstances, to educate
them ; for a campaign led by a narrow mind * will not succeed
[laughter], and still less will be performed the difficult duties
which the officer has toward his men, in order to keep their

---

* Bismarck plays on the word "*Thor*," meaning a man who is
almost a fool, and "*Thor*," a narrow door, through which no
army could pass to battle.

love and esteem. The kind of education which is necessary for that, and the executive ability which among us is generally shown by the officer in comradeship and a sense of honor, can be shown by no class of officers abroad, for no regulations or issued directions will impress it on them. Therein we are superior to every nation, and on that account they are not able to imitate us. [ "Bravo !"] So I am not anxious about it.

But, besides this, there is another advantage in your acceptance of this measure : the very strength for which we strive shows that we are inclined to peace. That sounds paradoxical, but it is true.

With such a powerful machine as we wish to make the German army, no one would undertake to attack us. If I were to stand here before you to-day and say to you,—supposing the conditions were different from what they are, according to my conviction,—"We are urgently threatened by France and Russia ; we can see that we shall be attacked by them ; according to my opinions as a diplomatist and as a military man, it will be more advantageous to us if we strike the first blow than if we act on the defensive,—that we *now attack at once,*—it will be more conducive to our success to wage an aggressive war, and I therefore beg the Reichstag for a loan of a milliard or of half a milliard in order to undertake immediate war against both our neighbors "—indeed, gentlemen, I do not know if you would have confidence enough in me to consent to that. I hope not. [Laughter.]

But if you had, it would not satisfy me. If we in Germany would wage a war with the full force of our national power, it must be a war in which all join, all bring sacrifices to it,—a war in which the whole nation must agree ; it must be a war of the people ; it must be a war conducted with the enthusiasm of 1870, when we were wickedly attacked.  I can still remember the shrill, joyful shouts at the Cologne railway-station : it was the same from Berlin to Cologne ; it was the same here in Berlin.  The waves of public opinion carried us into the war whether we would or no.  It must be so if the power of a people like ours is to arrive at its full worth.  But it would be very difficult to make the provinces understand now, to make the Confederate States and their populations understand, that war is inevitable, and must be.  It would be asked : " Indeed, are you so sure about it ?  Who knows ? "  In short, when we really came to begin to fight, the whole weight of prejudices and impossibilities would be much heavier than the material opposition with which we should be met by the enemy whom we attacked.  " Holy Russia " would be irritated at the onset.  France would bristle with arms as far as the Pyrenees.  It would be the same everywhere.  A war in which we were not backed by the consent of our people might be carried on, when at last the proper authorities considered it necessary to declare it ; it would be carried on sharply, and perhaps successfully, after fire and blood had once been seen: but it would not be radically fought, with that incentive and fire behind it which there would be in a war in which we had been attacked.  Then all Germany, from Memel to the Lake of Constance, would explode like a powder-mine, would bristle with arms, and no enemy would dare to venture to cope with the *furor Teutonicus* which would show itself at such an attack.  [" Bravo ! "]

If we are superior to our future opponents, as many military opinions besides our own acknowledge, we dare not let that superiority pass away from us.    Our military critics believe it ; naturally every soldier thinks it,—he would almost cease to be of service if he did not wish for war, and believe he would be successful in it.    If our rivals suppose it is fear of the issue which inclines us to peace, they err greatly. ["Quite right !"]    We trust as firmly to success in righteous matters as any lieutenant in a foreign garrison can trust to his third glass of champagne [laughter]—and perhaps on surer grounds.    Therefore it is not fear which inclines us to peace, but an accurate consciousness of our strength, the knowledge that should we be attacked at an unfavorable moment we are strong enough to resist it, and the consciousness that we can still leave it to God's providence to remove the necessity for war in the mean time.

Therefore we are not inclined for any kind of aggressive war, and if it can only originate by an attack from us it will not occur.    Fire must be kindled by some one ; we will not kindle it. ["Bravo !"]    Neither consciousness of our strength, as I have just described it, nor trust in our treaties, will prevent us from continuing our effort to preserve peace generally, with the same vigor as hitherto.    We will allow ourselves to be led by no ill-temper, and we will be governed by no dislike.    It is indeed true that the threats and insults, the challenges, which have been addressed to us, have excited an intense and natural animosity on our side ["Very true !"]—a difficult thing to do with Germans, for, as a nation, they are more impervious to being disliked than any other people. But we are taking pains to soothe these irritations, and we would strive for peace, now as ever, with our neighbors, but especially with Russia.    When I say, "especially with Russia," I am of the opinion that France offers us no security for the success of these endeavors, though I will not say that it does not try to; we will seek no quarrel, we will never attack France. We have always made very pleasant and friendly settlements of the many small incidents which the disposition of our neighbor to spy and to corrupt has caused, because I should consider it wicked for such fiddle-faddles to kindle a great national war, or to make one possible. There are cases where, it is said, the most reasonable give way. [Laughter.—" Very good ! "]

Therefore I name Russia by preference ; and I have the same confidence in the result,—about which I spoke a year ago, and which this "freethinking" paper has printed in such large type,—and that, too, without seeking for it,—or, as a German newspaper roughly expresses it, without "cringing" to Russia. That time is past; we no longer sue for love, either to France or Russia. ["Very good !"—Repeated "Bravo!"] The Russian press, Russian public opinion, has shown the door to an old, powerful, and faithful friend ; we will not obtrude ourselves. We have sought to win the old confidential relationship again, but we will run after no one. [Unanimous applause.] That does not disturb us ; ou the contrary, it is just one spur more why we should observe with redoubled exactness the claims of the Treaty which Russia has with us.

Among the clauses of the Treaty are some which are not acknowledged by all our friends : I mean, duties are included in it which we acquired toward Russia at the Berlin Congress in regard to Bulgaria, and which stood till 1885 quite undisputed. It is no question for me, who helped to prepare and signed the decisions of the Congress, because at that time we were all of opinion that the preponderating influence of Russia in Bulgaria should consent that Bulgaria, on its side, should give up Eastern Roumelia, thus reducing its population of 3,000,000 souls by some 800,000, because it gave satisfaction to the districts whose interests were involved. In consequence of this decision of the Congress, up to 1885 Russia appointed as prince a near relative of the Czar's family, of whom no one expected or could expect anything more than that he would be a faithful exponent of Russian policy. This policy appointed the Minister of War and a great number of officers ; in short, it ruled in Bulgaria ; there is no doubt about it.   The Bulgarians, or some of them, or their prince,—I do not know who,—were not contented with it. There was political stratagem ; a revolt from Russia took place.   From this has arisen a certain situation, which we have no call to remedy with force of arms, and which the claims upon us that Russia took home from the Congress cannot alter theoretically.   Whether, if Russia should assert its claims forcibly, other difficulties would arise in conjunction therewith, I do not know ; it does not concern us at all.   We will not support forcible means, nor advise them.   I do not think there is any inclination toward them,—I am comparatively certain that none exist.   But should Russia seek by diplomacy, through a suggestion, the interference of the Suzerain of Bulgaria, the Sultan,—if it try to obtain that, I hold it to be the task of a loyal German policy to abide clearly by the decision of the Berlin treaty, and by the interpretation we gave it when it was signed, without any exception, and on which I, at least, cannot mistake the opinions of the Bulgarians.   Bulgaria, the little country lying between the Danube and the Balkans, is certainly not an object of sufficient size to make it the cause, the reason, why Europe should plunge into a war from Moscow to the Pyrenees, and from the North Sea to Palermo, the issue of which nobody can foretell; at the end it would scarcely be known what the fighting had been about. [Laughter.]

I can therefore declare that the unfriendliness which we have experienced from Russian public opinion, and especially from the Russian press, will not prevent us, as soon as Russia expresses the wish, from diplomatically supporting the diplomatic steps which Russia may take in order to regain its interest in Bulgaria. I say designedly, "as soon as Russia expresses the wish." In former times we occasionally took the trouble to fulfill Russian wishes after receiving confidential intimations; but we have lived to see that Russian newspapers have found themselves immediately obliged to prove that those very steps of German policy were most hostile toward Russia, and have attacked us because we have been beforehand in the performance of Russian wishes. We did that at the Congress, but we shall not do it again. If Russia officially invites us to support steps for the restoration of the measures of Congress, providing for the situation in Bulgaria of the Sultan as suzerain, I do not hesitate to advise His Majesty to allow it. The treaties make this demand on our loyalty toward a neighbor, with whom, be public opinion what it will, we have to maintain a neighborly relationship, and defend great and mutual monarchical interests, such as the interests of order against all its antagonists in Europe. I do not doubt that the Czar of Russia will make war if he find that the interests of his great empire of a hundred million subjects compel him to. But these interests cannot possibly be such as to compel him to wage war against us; I do not consider it even probable that such a prescript of interests is at all imminent.

I do not, then, believe in an immediate impending disturbance of peace,—if I may recapitulate,—and beg that you will consider the measure in question quite independently of this thought, this apprehension, and regarded only as a full reestablishment of the employment of the power which God has given the German nation in case of need. Should we not need it, then we will not call upon it; and we will try to avoid the necessity of needing it.

This effort is, to some degree, made more difficult for us through threatening newspaper articles from abroad, and I wish to direct this warning principally to that country to discontinue these threats. They lead to nothing. The threatening which we get—not from the government, but from the press—is really an incredible stupidity [laughter], when it is remembered that a great and a proud power, such as the German Empire, is thought to be capable of being intimidated by a certain threatening formation of printers' ink—by a collection of words. ["Bravo!"] That should be discontinued; then it would be easier for us to meet both our neighbors more pleasantly. Every country is in some way eventually responsible for the watch it sets upon its press; the score is presented at any time in the form of the opinion of other countries. We can be easily bribed with love and kindness—perhaps too easily,—but certainly not with threats. ["Bravo!"]

*We Germans fear God, but nothing else in the world* [enthusiastic applause]; and it is the fear of God which causes us to love and cherish peace. Let him who breaks it in defiance be assured that the war-inspiring love of Fatherland, which in 1813 called the whole people of a then weak, small, and exhausted Prussia around the flag, is to-day the common property of the whole German nation. And he who would attack the German nation in any way will find it armed with unity—every warrior having the firm belief in his heart : *God will be with us !* [Great and continuous applause.]

# APPENDIX.

## TREATY BETWEEN GERMANY AND AUSTRIA HUNGARY.

*[Imperial and State Gazette, 3d February, 1888.]*

THE governments of Germany and of the Austria-Hungarian Monarchy have resolved upon the publication of their definite Treaty of October 7th, 1879, in order to end doubts which have been entertained on different sides of their purely defensive intentions, which are construed into different aims. The allied governments are guided in their policy by the endeavor to preserve peace : and, as much as possible to avert all disturbance of the same, they are persuaded that the promulgation of the contents of their Treaty will remove every doubt thereupon, and have therefore determined to publish the same. The text runs as follows :—

*Considering* that Your Majesties, the German Emperor, King of Prussia, and the Emperor of Austria, King of Hungary, do conceive it Your undeniable duty as Monarchs to care for the safety of Your empires and the peace of Your peoples under all conditions ;

*Considering* that both Monarchs will be in a condition to perform this duty more easily and more effectively through the firm cohesion of both empires, as in former standing alliances ;

*Considering,* finally, that no one can object to an intimate relationship between Germany and Austria-Hungary, which, however, is well fitted to consolidate European peace, originating with the Treaty of Berlin :

YOUR MAJESTIES, The EMPEROR of GERMANY,

and

The EMPEROR of AUSTRIA, KING of HUNGARY,

since You solemnly engaged to each other that You would at no time impute to the other's purely defensive proceedings an aggressive tendency of any kind, have resolved to unite in a treaty for peace and for mutual protection.

To this end have Your Imperial Highnesses appointed as Your plenipotentiaries : H. I. M. the German Emperor, the R. H. Ambassador in Extraordinary and Plenipotential General Lieutenant Prince Henry VII. of Reuss, etc., etc.; H. I. M. the Emperor of Austria, King of Hungary, the R. H. Privy Counselor, Premier and Minister of Foreign Affairs, Field-Marshal-Lieutenant Gyula Count Andrassy, of Esik-Szent-Kiralfy and Kraszna-Horka, etc.,—who have convened this day at Vienna, and after exchange of good and sufficient credentials have agreed as follows :

*Article I.*—Should one of the two Empires be attacked by Russia, against the expectations and against the sincere wish of both Royal contracting parties, the Royal contracting parties are pledged each to assist the other with the whole fighting force of their Empires, and, according to their ability to conclude peace only mutually and harmoniously.

*Article II.*—Should one of the Royal contracting parties be attacked by another power, the other Royal contractor hereby pledges himself not only not to assist the aggressor of his Royal ally, but, at the least, to observe a favorable neutral disposition toward his Royal ally. Should, however, in such a case, the aggressive power be supported by Russia, be it in the form of active co-operation, be it through military measures which threaten the aggressed, then will hold good in this case Article I, of this treaty, with its stipulated pledge of mutual assistance from the whole army, immediately in force, and the conduct of the war of the Royal contracting parties shall then be mutual till peace is unanimously concluded.

*Article III.*—In conformity with its peaceful character, and in order to avoid every misconstruction, this Treaty shall be held secret, and will be communicated to a third Power only with the consent of both parties, and according to special agreement.

Both Royal contracting parties hope that, according to the outspoken opinions of the Czar Alexander at the meeting in Alexandrowo, the preparations for war in Russia will not prove really threatening for You, and have, on this ground, no occasion for any communication. Should, however, this hope prove to be mistaken, contrary to expectation, the two Royal contracting parties would acknowledge it a duty of loyalty at least to give notice confidentially to the Czar Alexander that You must consider an attack on one of You equivalent to an attack on both of You.

In witness whereof have the ambassadors signed this treaty personally and affixed Your seals.

*Given at Vienna, October 7, 1879.*

H. VII. P. REUSS.            ANDRASSY.
[L. S.]                              [L. S.]

www.ingramcontent.com/pod-product-compliance
Lightning Source LLC
Chambersburg PA
CBHW020229030726
47497CB00009B/3012